"You can have my tent tonight," Jeff said, his voice cutting through Willa's torturous thoughts.

She looked up in astonishment. "No, I couldn't do that." She clamped down on her lip, regretting the words the instant they slipped out of her mouth. Of course she could! "Where would you sleep?" she asked softly, and berated herself for sounding like the cream puff Jeff believed her to be.

"Out here under the stars. I'll keep watch for the *predators*."

She glared at him, certain he was laughing at her. She could even see the laughter dancing in his eyes.

"Unless, of course, you'd rather keep watch," he said. "I understand you're pretty good with your feet."

"No, that's quite all right. You've seen one star, you've seen them all. But, thanks, I'll take you up on the tent offer."

"My pleasure." He leaned close, his warm breath tickling her ear and sending shivers straight down her spine. "Maybe in the morning you'll tell me exactly what you're doing here, Blondie."

CYNTHIA COOKE

Nine years ago, Cynthia Cooke lived a quiet, peaceful life, caring for her eighteen-month-old daughter, until she gave birth to boy/girl twins. Hip-deep in diapers and baby food, peacefulness gave way to chaos. She kept her sanity by reading romance novels and dreamed of someday writing one. She counts her blessings every day as she fulfills her dreams with the help of good friends, a supportive husband and three wild children who constantly keep her laughing and her world spinning. *Luck and a Prayer* is her debut novel.

LUCK AND A PRAYER

CYNTHIA COOKE

Published by Steeple Hill Books™

STEEPLE HILL BOOKS

ISBN 0-373-87248-8

LUCK AND A PRAYER

This edition published by arrangement with Steeple Hill Books.

Visit us at www.steeplehill.com

Printed in U.S.A.

A time to weep, and a time to laugh;
a time to mourn, and a time to dance.

—*Ecclesiastes* 3:4

To my friends: Gail Ranstrom, Nina Bruhns,
Michele Hauf and Pat White. You are the best!
Hugs to the ABC kids to being the great kids
you are, and to my own hunky hero, Dale,
for your unwavering support
and encouragement throughout the years.
I love you all.

A special thanks to Kim Nadelson and Tracy Farrell
for believing in *Luck and a Prayer* and making this
author's dreams come true.

Chapter One

Detective Willa Barrett stifled a groan as jolts of pain gnawed at her calves and moved up her spine. Grimacing, she shifted slightly, but stayed crouched behind the kitchen counter, not daring to move or make a sound.

Why Jack would bring someone in here at 9:00 a.m. was beyond her, especially after one of his late-night parties. Luckily, her brother Johnny had just left; otherwise, she'd have a hard time explaining why a ''paying customer'' was sleeping in the spare room.

''Nice, isn't it?'' Jack Paulson boomed from the other side of the counter. ''One of our best. You'll be rooming with Blondie,'' he told the woman. ''She'll take good care of you. Teach you everything you need to know.''

No doubt. Willa barely resisted snorting aloud. A roommate would make her farce of ''working'' all that more difficult. Now she'd actually have to take the other undercover cops into her room with her. A thought she didn't relish, since there wasn't one of them she could tolerate. Straining her ears, she tried to determine exactly where Jack and the woman were positioned.

She gnawed her bottom lip and rubbed her injured arm. She couldn't afford to get caught spying on Jack again. The captain had ordered her to go home and take care of her arm, but had she? No. Instead she'd hurried back to the strip dressed in purple sequins and tassels, swinging her hips in her exaggerated ''Blondie'' mode. Left and right she'd swung, calling to motorists, winking, hawking her feminine wares, clattering down Sunset Boulevard in five-inch spiked heels.

The same heels that were torturing her calf muscles now as she adjusted her weight from one hip to the other in her cramped position behind the counter. She had one last shot to get the goods on Jack Paulson and she wasn't about to lose it because the captain had gotten squeamish over a sprained arm and pulled her off the case. She couldn't worry about that now; right now the only thing that mattered was nailing Jack Paulson.

Willa turned on the special Pen Cam Johnny had acquired and inched it onto the counter behind a pot of African violets. The amazing little thing looked just like a standard ink pen, but in actuality was a self-contained video and audio outfit. It must have cost Johnny a pretty penny, but he was as anxious to put Mr. Slimebag Paulson behind bars as she was. They both had good reason.

Adjusting the Pen Cam's position, she hunkered back down. Perhaps now she should make her way back to the bedroom where she'd have less of a chance of getting caught.

"You sure are a pretty thing. Wear your hair loose for me. That's it, falling over your shoulders." Jack's raspy voice, low and seductive, filled the room. "What do you think of our new girl, Carlos?"

"She's a beauty, boss. She'll class up the place all right."

Silently, Willa shoved her back into the cabinets. Carlos sounded close. Too close. Jack was known far and wide for being cruel to his girls, but it wasn't Jack who did the most damage. It was Carlos. Jack just liked to watch.

"Here, you'll have your own place, your own money, you'll make your own rules," Jack continued his pitch to seduce his hapless victim into the "good" life. "I won't be here to check what time you come in or to tell you who you can see. If you want that kind of treatment, stay home with Daddy."

"You don't have to worry about me, sir." The woman's voice, soft and low, trembled as she spoke. "I won't give you any trouble."

Willa inched her way along the kitchen counter toward her room, once again trying to get a handle on Jack's position. She'd feel better if she could make it out of the kitchen. That way she could come out of a door when he called her, instead of popping up from behind the counter like a peeping Willa-in-the-box.

"All I want from you in return is sixty percent, Tracey. That will cover your expenses. This is a nice place—it ain't cheap. Is it, Carlos?"

"No, sir. Not cheap at all," Carlos's voice thundered, resonating right down Willa's spine.

The creep was directly above her. With knees burning and calves screaming, Willa quickly scampered along the counter to the other side of the kitchen. She wouldn't make it back to her room now. From Carlos's position, he'd be able to see her. She'd have to stay and hope Jack didn't call for her.

"I know you're not experienced with this kind of life, so I'll do you a favor. I'll give you a few days to get used to the place. I'll send you to a few parties; let you meet the rest of the girls. See, old Jack isn't such a bad guy," he said heartily. His chuckle turned Willa's stomach. "You'll love it here. All my girls love working for Jack Paulson. Don't they, Carlos?"

"Yes, sir. They sure do."

"You see, Tracey, my job is to make sure we both earn a lot of money while having a great time doing it. Life's too short not to have fun, don't you agree?" He paused. "But most of all, I enjoy taking care of you girls. Nothing bad ever happens to one of Jack's girls. That's a God-given promise."

Willa rolled her eyes at the manure spewing from his lips, and wondered how Jack defined the word *bad.* No one with a brain could be buying this garbage. She peeked around the corner and almost choked. The girl sitting across from him couldn't be more than twelve or thirteen. Good Lord! Where had he found a baby like her? This was sinking to an all-time low, even for Jack.

The girl's eyes widened as they met Willa's. Biting back a groan, Willa swung back behind the counter.

''Here's five hundred to get you started,'' Jack stated. ''Go buy yourself some new clothes and a few knickknacks for your room, something to make this place feel like home. It's all yours now.''

''Yes, sir,'' the girl said. ''Thank you.''

''You'll pay me back by being a good girl and working hard. Jack's girls know how to get ahead. Blondie will show you the ropes. Where is she anyway, Carlos? She should be here to meet the newest member of our team.'' The dinette chair scraped across the wooden floor. ''Hey, Blondie,'' Jack yelled.

Willa bit her lip, and wished she could sink into the floor.

''Um, sir?'' the girl spoke up, nabbing Jack's attention. ''Will I—that is, will I ever be able to visit my friends?''

The girl's lilting voice broke Willa's heart. Don't worry, sweetie, she thought. I'll get you out of this. Just as soon as I get myself out from behind this counter.

''You're a runaway, Tracey. I'm giving you a place to live, a new identity, a way to support yourself, and start-up money. Now why would you want to blow all that by contacting your friends or family? You're going to make a whole bunch of new friends right here. We're your family now.'' The front door opened. ''Come on, doll,'' Jack said. ''Let me show you around.''

Willa fell back against the cupboards and stretched out her aching legs as she heard the door click shut. She'd done it! She'd gotten the whole conversation on videotape. This time, nothing could stop Jack Paulson from paying for a very long time.

''I thought you learned your lesson the last time I caught you spying on the boss.'' Carlos's raw hate-filled voice slithered around her.

Willa cringed. She stood, rocking unsteadily in her five-inch heels and faced him eye to eye, ignoring the glacial chill quivering down to her toes. ''I don't know what you're talking about, Carlos.''

He grabbed her by the shoulders, his bony fingers biting into her flesh. ''You were eavesdropping on the boss.''

His breath, smelling of coffee and cigarettes, nearly gagged her. ''I wasn't, Carlos. Really. I was just waiting for Jack to leave so we could be alone. That's all.'' She lifted a painted nail to his chin and flicked the stubble he thought made him look sexy instead of just slimy.

He loosened his grasp, then pushed her against the counter. ''I knew you liked me,'' he rasped.

''Of course I do, sugar,'' she lied with a honey-thickened tongue. ''If you give me a little time, I'll prove it to you.''

''I've got time.''

The way he looked at her sent a fresh round of shudders coursing down her back. He turned toward her room. Not able to wait another second, she snatched up the pen. He turned back, staring at the Pen Cam in her hand, suspicion crossing his face.

''Did you really think I'd fall for that act?''

Fear hammered in her chest, but she was careful to

make sure it didn't show on her face. "Which act is that, sugar?"

With two easy strides, he was on her and reaching for the pen. She pulled away, palming it behind her back. With spring-loaded speed, he grabbed her arm and jerked the Pen Cam from her grasp. "What's this?"

She didn't answer, just held her breath and prayed the man was as dumb as he looked. He started to unscrew the pen's barrel.

"Don't—" she said softly.

"Don't what?" He dropped the Pen Cam to the floor and raised a steel-toed boot.

The closest she'd ever come to nailing Jack Paulson was recorded on that pen and she wasn't about to let some moronic flunkie pulverize it. She swung back, brought up one leg and—"Whaaa chai!"—kicked with all her might. Five inches of pointy heel dug deep into soft flesh.

Grunting, he doubled over. She reached down, grabbed the pen, then clattered as fast as she could out the door and down the hall toward the stairs. She had to get the pen to the captain. It was the only way to stop Jack, to save that young girl and to save herself another night of knowing that animal was still out there spreading his poison and infecting everything he touched.

He's finally going to pay, Daddy. Just like I promised.

She ran toward the staircase at the end of the hall, pushing herself harder, faster. One spiked heel caught an uneven board. She slipped, twisting her ankle as she fought for balance. Through the fog of pain, she kept moving. It wasn't bad enough to stop her. For that, she'd have to be dead.

"I'm going to kill you, woman!"

If only she had time to lose the stilettos. They'd make a mighty fine weapon in her hand, but on her feet they were downright deadly. A door two apartments down opened. If she could reach it and lock herself in, she might have enough time to call for backup.

Betty Jones, one of Jack's oldest pros, stepped into the hall. "Hey, Blondie! What's up?"

Without a word, Willa raced past her, slammed shut her door and threw the bolt. She dashed for the phone and dialed 911.

"Blondie, open up!" Betty yelled, her feeble fists hitting the door.

"Nine-one-one emergency," the voice on the line answered.

"I need help...."

With one earth-shattering kick, the door flew open, slamming against the wall, shredding the plaster. She had to find a weapon! Dropping the phone, Willa slipped around the counter into the kitchen and yanked open the drawer she kept her knives in back in her apartment. She stared blankly at potholders and dishtowels. "Blast!"

"Give it up, Blondie. You're mine now." With slow deliberate steps, Carlos walked into the kitchen, cornering her against the sink. "Take a walk, Betty," he called without checking to see if she listened. He knew she would obey, and so did Willa. His gaze locked on hers. The expression on his face was downright animalistic.

All her years of training on the force scattered right out of her mind. This man was pure demented evil. He wrapped his hands around her waist, picked her up and threw her across the kitchen counter. She landed on the floor, the impact jolting every bone in her body. Within seconds, he was on her.

She groped blindly around her and with splayed fingertips, felt the telephone she'd dropped to the floor. With white-knuckle ferocity, she grasped the phone and swung it against his head. He clutched his temple and fell to the side. It was the second she needed. She was up and running again. Her only hope for safety was to reach the boulevard cluttered with people, traffic and cops.

''Run, little girl! Faster or you'll never escape me!'' His bellow echoed down the hall as he sprinted after her. She didn't look back. Didn't have to. His labored breath bounced off the walls in the narrow stairwell, his heavy boots clobbered the stairs behind her, all signs that he was closing in fast.

The door to the street loomed ahead of her. Sunshine filtered through dirty glass—her light at the end of a dark tunnel. Ten feet. Seven.

If she could just make it out that door…

She felt his hand brush her shoulder and wrap itself in her hair. Her bleached-blond wig shifted, but held, the pins digging mercilessly into her scalp.

Five feet. Three.

His growl, bubbling like toxic laughter in his throat was close, too close. Panic swallowed her. She hit the door with all her strength, swinging it open. Sunshine burned her eyes. She'd made it! Her heart soared. Carlos's hand closed on her shoulder, pulling her off balance.

She tripped, falling, reeling into the white-hot sun, into safety. Strong arms roughly caught her before she hit the pavement. She looked up at her savior and stared into the reptilian eyes of Jack Paulson.

Jeff MacPhearson's fingers tightened on the steering wheel of the church van as he turned right onto Sunset Boulevard. The knot sitting in the bottom of his stomach grew as he took in the familiar sights of the street. Six blocks down, hang a right, then a left, and he'd be back at the old parish—his first parish, the parish of his greatest accomplishments and his biggest failure.

He pushed down the anger burgeoning within him. Tracey wasn't Dawn. This situation was completely different. He would find Tracey and bring her back home. He would not lose another child to these wicked streets, and yet, here he was, back in the place he'd fought so hard to get out of. Back on the dirty streets he'd struggled night after night to push from his mind by moving to a cleaner parish, a safer city. Back on Sunset Boulevard staring his personal demon in the face.

The swish of long brown hair caught his eye. He hit the brakes, ignoring the horn blaring behind him and stared at a familiar-looking brunette in a ridiculously tight miniskirt. She turned at the commotion and gave him a beckoning smile. He blew out a sigh of relief. She wasn't Tracey, though she wasn't much older than Tracey and he couldn't help feeling sorry for her, for all the girls that ended up on the strip.

He drove another block, then two, scanning the sidewalks on either side, searching every face, every lithe form for the missing thirteen-year-old. *"Please, Lord, please help me find her,"* he prayed, and then he spotted her, standing at the mouth of an alley, talking to a man who looked slimier than a used-car salesman at a clearance sale. Jeff did a double take. Jack Paulson! The old goat wrapped a meaty arm around her slim waist and led her toward the entrance of a two-story apartment building. Jeff stiffened his grip on the wheel, gathering the strength to stop himself from steering the van toward them and running the cretin down. The man deserved that and so much more.

"Keep your filthy hands off her," he hollered at the windshield, while desperately searching for a parking place. Careful not to lose sight of her, he pulled into a parking lot a quarter-mile down the street, jumped out of the van and ran toward them.

He could see the man's hand cupping Tracey's little elbow, could see his white teeth gleaming as he smiled down at her. Jeff pushed harder, fighting back the urge to call her name, to stop her from entering that building.

He couldn't imagine what had happened to make her choose the ungodly boulevard over her family home, but whatever it had been he could fix it. And whatever it was, he'd make it right this time. He had to, or what was the point? God hadn't chosen him to work with kids just to play volleyball. He was here to make a difference, to reach these kids, to show them the way to God's love and a healthy life.

One more block to go.

The building's door swung open and a platinum blonde in form-fitting purple spandex flew out the door and fell directly into the man with Tracey. Tracey jumped back.

''Blondie!'' Jack yelled as the woman slipped through his grasp and headed toward Jeff. Jack followed, leaving Tracey alone and giving Jeff the chance he'd been praying for. He lifted a hand and waved. Tracey's eyes widened as she saw him, her gaze locking on his. Come on, Tracey. Let me help you, he pleaded silently.

Something slammed into him, knocking him flat to the ground. The concrete packed a wallop to the back of his head. Bright stars of pain danced before his eyes and he couldn't find his breath.

The stars receded yet still he couldn't see. Something dry and sticky filled his mouth; something soft and curvy filled his hand. He jerked his hand off the silky spandex and spat out a mouthful of fake hair. ''Get off me, please,'' he groaned and at the same moment inhaled the sweet scent of vanilla and cream. He was breathing again and the woman smelled wonderful, not exactly what he'd expect from someone with her questionable taste in clothing.

''Sorry,'' she mumbled, and quickly righted her skewed wig. Curly wisps of red hair hung down from her temples mixing with the acrylic platinum waves. As she shifted, he felt a tug in his back pocket before her hipbone ground into his stomach. He groaned again.

''Thank the Lord above,'' he muttered, as she finally rose off him.

''Come on, Blondie,'' a deep voice said. ''We have some business upstairs.''

Jack yanked her to his side. ''Sorry, Jack,'' she said with a saucy smile. ''But I can't. I've already got an appointment and it ain't with you.''

''It is now.'' He pulled her arm up behind her back. She winced and leaned forward, but didn't make a sound.

''Hey,'' Jeff protested, and started to rise, then fell back, shaking the momentary dizziness from his head.

''Jeff, are you all right?'' Tracey kneeled next to him, her big, brown still-innocent eyes full of concern.

''You know this guy, Tracey?'' Jack asked.

She turned to him, biting her lower lip. ''Um, yes, sir. He's the pastor at my church.''

Brushing off the pain, Jeff rose to his feet and dropped a protective hand on Tracey's shoulder.

''Church, heh?'' Jack chuckled, though his eyes gleamed with menace as they took in Jeff's gesture.

She nodded. ''Uh-huh, in Pasadena.''

''You're a little out of your neighborhood, aren't you, Padre?''

''Just here to pick up my girl,'' Jeff said, and turned away from him and made strong eye contact with Tracey. She had a hard time holding his gaze, but his didn't waver. ''We're going backpacking, remember? Everyone is waiting for you.''

''You wouldn't believe what I caught Blondie doin'

this time, boss.'' Another man, huge and brooding, grabbed the woman's arm.

''Take her upstairs and see that she doesn't get away,'' Jack growled.

The woman's green eyes met Jeff's, surprising him with their fiery determination. This was a woman who could take care of herself. And yet... ''Do you need help, miss? I'd be happy to give you a lift anywhere you want to go. Anywhere,'' he emphasized.

The brute holding her burst out laughing.

''She can't make it and neither can Tracey.'' Jack took a step toward them, his face set in stone. Jeff gave Tracey's shoulder a protective squeeze. ''I believe that decision is up to the ladies.''

''Not anymore. I'm taking care of Tracey now and I can do it a whole lot better than the rest of you hypocrites.''

Fury swelled in Jeff's chest. This animal preyed on lost women and children and he wouldn't get his filthy paws on one of *his* kids. He'd die first. He took Tracey's small shoulders in his hands and faced her, blocking Jack from her view. ''Give me a chance, Tracey. Please. I'll make everything all right at home. I promise.'' His gut wrenched as fear and confusion flashed though her eyes. *Please, God, let me have the chance to make it right this time. Don't let me lose another child.*

''Come on, Jack. Let the kid go,'' the woman interrupted. ''I thought you said we've got business.''

Jack sneered at her. ''Like you're worth it, Blondie.''

With lightning speed, she pivoted and brought up

her knee—hard. The brute holding her doubled over, releasing his grasp. She jerked free, spun one hundred and eighty degrees, and kicked Jack's granite face in rapid succession. Jeff almost cheered aloud.

Tracey groaned.

Blondie turned and to his astonishment gave them both a shove. "Run!" she urged.

Jeff didn't waste a second. He grabbed Tracey by the hand and hauled her down the street toward the van. Within minutes they were locked inside and he was pulling onto the boulevard. He expected the woman in spandex would have disappeared, but there she was holding her own with Jack's man. One lithe leg kicked high, knocking the brute in the chin.

"She's amazing," he said, awestruck.

"Unbelievable," Tracey murmured. Jeff turned to his passenger tucked safe and secure in her seat belt and said a quick prayer of thanks, though he knew his job had only just begun. A squad car screeched to a stop in front of the apartment building as Jeff pulled past them. He glanced at his watch and then at Tracey. "If we hurry, we can still make it to our campsite by nightfall. Are you game?"

She looked at him, then quickly averted her gaze. He heard a soft "Sure," and, for now, that was enough.

"Good, now call your mother. Tell her you're sorry for worrying her half to death, then let me talk to her."

Reluctantly, she took the phone. When she handed it back to him, he asked Mrs. Wilcox if he could still take Tracey camping with the others. "I think it will be good for her," he added.

Luckily, she agreed.

At least for a few more days she'd be safe, and he'd have time to talk to her without distractions and reminders of what had happened here today. Perhaps then he'd find out what had gone wrong at home and he'd have his chance to put her back on the right path.

Willa scowled as the van with Morning Star Church printed across its door drove away. She succumbed to the officers on patrol as they read her her rights, then let them cuff her and throw her into the back of the squad car. Another car appeared to take Jack Paulson and Carlos downtown.

''Thanks, guys,'' she muttered as they pulled into traffic. She stretched her aching shoulders and tried to ignore the pinch of the cuffs on her wrists. ''You could have been a little gentler, though.''

''Hey, we wouldn't want to blow your cover, Blondie,'' Rick snickered behind the wheel. ''The way you were moving them heels—whooeee, speed lightning.''

''Yeah, I wouldn't want to face you in a dark alley,'' his partner, Cliff added.

''Honey, if you don't loosen these cuffs, you're not gonna want to face me anywhere.''

''Whoa, retract those claws.'' Rick laughed. ''Believe me, those cuffs are the least of your problems.''

''What d'ya mean?''

''Captain's waiting for you at headquarters and he's not too hunky dory. Says he wants you in his office looking very contrite within twenty minutes and if I were you, I'd lose the wig.''

Willa cringed. She'd directly disobeyed an order

from her captain. She'd be facing desk duty for sure now. "Hey, guys. Do me a favor and say I split. You can drop me on the corner."

They both burst out laughing. She knew what they thought of her. *Obsessed* and *cracked up* were just a few of the terms she'd heard whispered around the department. It didn't matter. She'd show them.

Jack Paulson should have been put behind bars a long time ago for killing her father. He hadn't been. Now it was up to her to see that he was. And, this time, she finally had the evidence to put him away. Unfortunately, it was tucked in the back pocket of that cute pastor's jeans. She took a deep breath. As soon as she got it back, she'd have Jack right where she wanted him.

But first she had to deal with Ben. And Captain Ben Armstrong was not pleasant to be around when he'd been crossed.

Chapter Two

At her locker, Willa quickly changed out of her hooker outfit, dragged on a pair of jeans and a LAPD T-shirt, wiped her face clean with one of those instant makeup removers, and pulled her hair back into a ponytail. She jogged on canvas shoes that didn't make a sound to the captain's office and silently slipped into a chair across from his desk.

He lowered a handful of reports and glowered at her. ''Well?''

''It's Saturday, Captain. Technically, I'm off duty.''

''Then technically, I can have you locked up for assault and disturbing the peace.''

''Yeah, I suppose you could.''

''Yeah.'' The word hung suspended between them.

''But you won't.'' She cocked him an elfish grin.

His expression hardened. ''I pulled you from the Paulson case. In fact, I distinctly remember telling you to go home and rest that arm. In no uncertain terms, I warned you to stop your renegade antics.''

"Yes, sir, you did."

Captain Ben Armstrong leaned forward in his chair and scrutinized her. It was a hard look, and one she still hadn't grown accustomed to no matter how many times he'd directed it her way. She shifted and bit her lower lip, swallowing the defensiveness rising in her chest.

His tone softened. "I want to help you, Willa. Really I do. I know what getting this guy means to you, and I think you know what it would mean to me, but your obsession is impacting my department."

A spring tightened in Willa's back. "Obsession?"

"Do you deny it? How many times have you gone back to that apartment alone without even bothering to check in? And word on the street has it your brother's been there, too."

"Johnny has as much right to Paulson's throat as I do." Even though he'd been older than her twelve years at the time of their father's death, Johnny took it even harder than she did. No matter what Ben said, no matter how close he'd been to her family over the years, he would never understand what it had been like for them to suddenly lose the strongest force in their lives.

She had to give Ben credit for trying, but a surrogate dad could never replace what they'd lost. Her dad had been everything to them, the one who was home most days when they got home from school, the one who helped them with their homework, bandaged their bruises and dried their tears. How she longed to have him sit across the table from her and smile as she relayed the events of her day. Even just one more time.

"The bottom line, Captain, is that I'm doing what I have to do to get the job done."

He took a deep breath. "There are a lot of ways to get the job done, you've chosen the one you've decided works best for you."

"Your point?"

"You need to start doing what's best for the department. *If* you want to continue working here."

Willa's eyes narrowed.

"There isn't an officer in this precinct that will work with you," he continued, treading deeper into uncharted waters. "They don't trust you will be there for them when the chips are down."

Like you were for my dad? Her teeth wrestled a grasp on her tongue to keep the long-unsaid words from escaping.

"You refuse to play by the rules or follow directions. We are a team here and you need to be a part of it. Out of loyalty and an obligation to your dad's memory, I've given you more warnings than you've deserved, but now you've left me no choice. I'm pulling you off the street."

"You're what?" Incredulity rose in her voice. "I'm the best cop you've got."

"You're a loose cannon, and one of these days you're going to get someone besides yourself hurt."

Willa's self-control skittered out the door. "You can't take me off the street. I've got it this time. I've got evidence that Jack is serving up young girls—*babies*—as the main course at his twisted dinner parties. He's moved onto prepubescent girls. I can't let him do it. This has gone way beyond what he's done to my family.''

''What kind of evidence?'' he said, portraying no outward reaction to what she'd just told him. Surely, he couldn't be that cold, that jaded.

''A videotape. I got it on one of those cameras that look like a pen.''

''One of Johnny's gadgets, I presume. Hand it over, then go see Donna about a desk duty schedule,'' he dismissed her, burying his nose back into his paperwork.

''I can't.''

Exasperated, he looked up and let out a deep sigh.

''I don't have it.''

''You've just rambled on about evidence you don't have? Why are you wasting my time, Willa?''

''I had it. And I'll have it back in an hour, tops!''

''Where is it?''

''I ditched it in a minister's back pocket.''

''You what!''

''I had to get rid of it. Carlos knew something was up with the pen and I couldn't take the chance of losing it.''

''So, you put a civilian in jeopardy? And a minister at that! You never should have gone back into that apartment without backup. This just proves my point, Willa.''

''No, it doesn't. It proves that I'm the one with the guts to roll around in the manure and not let the stink do me in. I'm the one who got the goods on Jack and you'll have the evidence as soon as I get it back from the Morning Star Church in Pasadena.''

Without a word the captain picked up the phone. "Send whoever is closest over to the Morning Star Church in Pasadena. I need one of those camera pens picked up from a minister. No, no name, but he was on the strip this morning. Can't be more than one up there. I want a call as soon as we have it."

"Then we bring Jack down," she said triumphantly.

"So what?" he answered, his tired eyes void of emotion. "There are a hundred more Jack Paulsons ready to take his place."

"And I'll get them, too. But first, this slimeball is going to pay for killing my dad."

The captain scrubbed his face with his hands. "I want you to see Louis."

"I'm not seeing a shrink."

"I told your mother fifteen years ago you needed counseling. Margo and I have lost countless night's sleep worrying about you and the decisions you've made. We've done everything we could think of to help you, especially after your mother died, too. We even abided by your wishes when you refused counseling. But by God, I'm going to make sure you get it now."

A deep well of long-lived frustration bubbled inside her. "I told you then and I'm telling you now, I don't need to see a shrink."

"You need to get over your father's death or you'll never be the cop you want to be. You'll never be the person you can be. When was the last time you had a personal commitment to anybody or anything other than Jack Paulson?"

"Leave my personal life out of it."

"That should be easy since you don't have one."

Cold fury froze Willa's heart. "I'm the cop I want to be, now."

"You'll never be a good one, Willa."

"I am good."

He slammed both fists on his desk. "No! You're not. As of right now, you're a desk jockey. And if you ever want to get away from the phones, you'll see Louis, and you'll continue to see him until he gives you a clean bill of health."

"I won't!" Willa jumped to her feet. The aluminum chair crashed to the floor behind her.

Ben scowled. "You will, or you're out of here."

"You wouldn't do that to me."

"Watch me."

Willa bit back some choice words as the phone rang. Stunned, she stared at it, trying to catch her breath and calm her temper as she righted the overturned chair.

His lips tightened into a straight line as he banged the receiver into its cradle. "Your so-called evidence has headed for the hills."

"What?"

"Your minister took a bunch of kids backpacking through Sequoia."

Willa collapsed back into the chair. "Sequoia? As in National Forest?"

"Yep, and seeing how you're the only one who knows what the poor man looks like, you're going to be the one to find him. I think a day or two in the wilderness will be good for you."

"Wilderness?" Willa ignored the dread settling in

the pit of her stomach. ''You mean out there in the woods where the bears live?'' She'd rather take on the animals stalking the strip.

''If you'd prefer, you can spend the rest of the weekend hitting the phones. Take your pick.''

''Fine, fine. I'm off. Gone. I'll enjoy myself, I'm sure. Fresh air and all that.''

He looked at his watch. ''I'll expect you back Monday night with evidence that better knock my socks off.''

''Yep, sure thing.''

He handed her a slip of paper. ''Here's the name of the youth director that has the trails and campsites where you'll find the pastor. I suggest you get a hotel in the area and try to catch them in the morning. You'll never make it to the campsite before nightfall.''

''No problem. And Captain, after you see that poor little girl on the tape, you'll be glad I stopped him.'' Silently she added, *Then you'll rethink this whole desk-jockey shrink thing. I know you will.*

By midafternoon, Willa was navigating the winding mountain road as if she'd been doing it all her life, not at all put off by the narrowing turns or the tall poles with painted red tops lining the sides of the road. Snow poles, the man at the service station had said. She shuddered. The very idea of being stuck in this place with that much snow on the ground made her turn down the air conditioner. She'd only seen snow once as a child, before her dad had died, when life had still been full of promise and happy days.

She glanced over at the new backpack sitting in the

passenger seat. The man at Oshman's had given her everything she'd need and more, even a new pair of hiking boots. She was all set, though she wasn't sure why she'd bothered. They couldn't have had that much of a head start on her. How far could one guy and six kids get? She'd have them tracked down within an hour, she reasoned.

A half hour later, she pulled into the campground parking lot and parked next to the church van. "Gotcha," she said, smiling, then swung the pack onto her back and stretched her shoulder blades, at once thankful for the intense workout sessions she'd recently added to her routine. "This thing's heavy," she grumbled aloud, suddenly sure that salesman had sold her a lot more junk than she actually needed.

She stopped at the bottom of the hill and read the trail markers. There were several, offering paths for beginners to the more stringent superadvanced levels. She took out the sheet of paper the youth director of the church had given her with the proper trails marked.

Obviously, this pastor was no stranger to the woods. He started with an easy trail, then moved on to different ones, each rising in intensity as they moved deeper into the backcountry. Oh well, she was in shape. She didn't spend three hours a week on the treadmill for nothing.

Two hours later, Willa's thigh muscles burned with a fire she'd never before felt as she plodded up the hill, and no matter how hard she tried, she couldn't seem to push enough air into her painfully constricted lungs. She stopped on a rock, took a swig off the water bottle from her pack and examined her notes one more time. There was no way she could be lost. They must have gotten a bigger head start than she thought.

She stood, groaned, pulled back her aching shoulders, then set out again. How could Ben say those things to her? She had a life. How many times had she sat at his dinner table and told him and Margo about the things she was doing? She shopped, she read, she jogged. She loved her fitness classes. She'd met a few people at the gym and had even dated a Neanderthal or two. "I'm just a very focused person," she muttered. "Very focused on Jack."

She swatted another bee out of her face. Lord, she hated the woods—the dirt, the incessant noise, the swishing of the trees and bushes. And to think people actually did this for fun. What she wouldn't give for the corner booth in Starbucks and a large iced tea with a lemon slice floating on the top.

She dragged a hand across her damp forehead. Where could they be? How many miles had she walked? By the aching soreness in her tootsies, she guessed at least a hundred. She groaned as she crested the top of yet another hill. She couldn't take any more. Not one more step. Slipping out of her pack, she stumbled into a lush, green meadow, fell flat on her back in the thick grass, and stared up at the blindingly blue sky.

Her throbbing muscles and bones settled into the soft earth. *Oh, this feels good.* When at last her breathing slowed and her body stopped creaking, she sat up and yanked off her brand-new, not-so-spiffy boots. Broken skin stuck to cotton as she pulled her sock mercilessly away from her foot. Her feet, red and swollen, were needled with broken blisters.

''Oh, no,'' she moaned, and wished she'd stuck with her tennies. She took another swig of water, then glanced at her watch. She'd been tromping around for two and a half hours and she still hadn't seen hide nor hair of one youth minister and six kids. She feared she might be on the wrong trail after all, or even the wrong mountain.

Then she heard something.

Her heart stilled. It's nothing, she told herself. I'm hearing things. She sat up straighter and looked through the tall grass, trying to determine what the rustling sound could be. About ten feet away the green blades parted, billowing slightly, then falling down in quick succession toward her.

Willa screamed. She jumped up, then back, tripped over a discarded boot, and fell right back on her derriere.

The thing in the grass was still coming at her, faster and faster. Crab crawling, she scurried backward away from the slithering reptile, screaming again, demanding that it get away from her and breathing so hard she feared her lungs might explode.

Behind her, the bushes shook with the ferocity of a 7.0 quake. Good Lord, she'd roused a bear! Terror leaped into her arrhythmic heart and stopped it cold.

''What? What is it?'' A masculine voice demanded. Not a huge furry brown thing after all, but a man—a fine-looking pastor whose sultry-smooth voice jump-started her heart and pushed the air back into her lungs. At least until it whooshed out again in appreciation of those wonderfully broad shoulders.

"A s-s-s—" She couldn't say the word. Hyperventilating, she frantically searched the grass for the slithering monster.

"A snake?"

"Yes, uh-huh." She nodded, vigorously.

"Okay." He searched the grass. "It's gone. You scared it away. You'll be fine," he said casually, too casually considering she almost lost her life. He gestured toward the area of flattened grass and her discarded socks and boots. "You really shouldn't lie down in the middle of a grassy field."

She guessed not.

He stared down at her bare feet. "Those look pretty nasty. Can you walk?"

"Of course I can walk. I can go anywhere as long as I get out of here."

He laughed; the deep warm sound resonated in his wide chest. She liked it. It sounded real, genuine and totally foreign to her. Sunshine glinted off sun-streaked hair and a sparkle twinkled in his eyes. Eyes as brilliant as that blindingly blue sky above her. She didn't think it right that anyone should have eyes that color, or that it'd look so good on a mere mortal. And why on earth did she have goose bumps on her arms?

"All right, then. We're camped not far from here. If you want, you can rest there and fix up your feet."

"Thanks. I'd appreciate that. You don't know how much. For a minute, I wasn't sure I'd ever see a living, breathing, life-saving human being ever again." *Let alone one nature-loving heart-stopping youth minister.*

His grin tilted.

She zipped her lips, then smiled back, wide and foolish. She couldn't help it. His crooked little grin was infectious and she couldn't believe he'd found *her.*

His gaze slowly perused her face. "I know this sounds crazy way up here, but have we met? I can't put my finger on it, but there's something familiar about you."

"Nope. Can't say that we have," she lied, suppressing a guilty twinge. They hadn't, she told herself, at least not technically. She'd decided on the trek up there that the best course of action would be to go incognito, grab the pen and get out. If that poor girl was on the brink of falling into a life on the streets, the last thing she needed was for all her peers to discover what she'd already done—or had been about to do, she amended, hoping for the best. Who knew what the girl had told the preacher man. No need to make things more difficult for her than they already were.

"Welcome to our little corner of paradise." He easily swung her pack onto his back, for which she was more grateful than she cared to admit, and led her out of the field. She picked up her boots and followed as quickly as she could, but found herself wincing each time she took a step. How would she ever get back down off this mountain? She played with the idea of getting the captain to airlift her out, but he was still mad at her, and then she would have to admit she couldn't handle a few hiking trails and a little wilderness.

Maybe she could get this handsome man to carry

her down. She smiled at the thought while watching him walk ahead of her. She lost her smile as she hobbled into the circle of tents and saw the expectant faces of six kids.

"Everyone, I want you to meet a fellow packer." The pastor turned to her. "Sorry, I didn't catch your name."

She held out her hand. "Willa Barrett."

"Miss Willa Barrett."

Willa turned to the kids and plastered on a be-gentle-with-me-I'm-clueless-about-kids smile. They all greeted her warmly, all except the girl she'd taped selling her soul to Jack Paulson. Wariness narrowed the girl's big, brown eyes. Surely she didn't recognize her? If not yet, chances were good she would soon. Better to find the camera and get off this mountain as quickly as possible, before one youth minister and six scrub-faced innocents became entangled in the ugly side of life.

"Make yourself at home," the pastor said, pointing to a chair.

A real canvas chair. Cleopatra's throne wouldn't have looked so good. After her tortuous hike up the mountain, their camp had the makings of a four-star resort. Seven small tents nestled in a cluster of pines surrounded a fire pit. The kids sat around it, resting on rocks and blankets.

"Wow, look at your feet." A boy no more than thirteen stood before her staring down at her swollen toes.

She wiggled them. "Yeah, new boots," she offered weakly, then collapsed into the chair.

"I have a first aid kit, if you'd like." His cheeks turned a soft crimson as he pushed his glasses farther up on his nose.

She smiled at his awkwardness. "Yes, thank you. I'd like."

"Good." He turned and walked toward the green tent closest to them and started digging through his pack.

"I'm Jeff MacPhearson," her rescuer offered. "We're all on an outing from the Morning Star Church. I'm the youth minister there."

"It's nice to meet you all. I'm certainly lucky you came along when you did."

"Especially since it will be getting dark soon."

Willa looked up at the sky; it didn't look anywhere near dark to her.

"You can set up camp here with us, if you'd like."

"Here?" Willa looked at the dirt-encrusted ground and the multitudes of little-legged things crawling all over it.

"You did bring a tent, didn't you?" He glanced toward her overstuffed pack lying where he'd dropped it.

"No, I don't think I did." She tried to remember the list of items the clerk had stuffed into the pack. She didn't remember a tent being among them. "I wasn't planning on staying an hour let alone the night," she explained, then shuddered. She'd have to sleep out here, at night, in the dark, with all those beady-eyed creatures watching from the trees and scurrying along the ground.

"Have you ever been backpacking before?" he

asked. There it was—laughter in his voice. She swung her gaze from the dark depths of the trees and met the twinkle in his eyes head-on.

"Sure, lots of times," she said, stiffening her back. There she was, lying again. And to a pastor no less. Although she had to admit he didn't look like a pastor. At least not any pastor she'd ever conjured up. She took in his muscular legs, wide chest, and strong, tanned arms. Nope. More like a construction worker. She could easily picture him with a hammer in his hand. A very large hammer.

"Found it!" The rosy-cheeked boy held up the first-aid kit in triumph.

"Thanks, Charles," Jeff said, and took the kit from him. Willa smiled as the boy shuffled his feet and spent an unusual amount of time studying the ground beneath them. She would never understand kids.

Bending before her, Jeff lifted her foot. She jumped at the unexpected contact, causing her chair to tilt. "Oh!" With her right hand, she braced herself, taking all her weight on her already sprained arm. Pain shot through her as her arm gave out.

"Whoa, there." Jeff caught her just before she fell, his hands on either side of her grasping the arms of her chair. She couldn't tell if it was from the shock, the pain or this incredibly handsome man's close proximity, but what had happened to her breath?

"Are you all right?"

"Yes," she muttered, unable to tear her gaze away from him. "It's a sprain, is all."

"I was only going to put antibiotic ointment on your blisters."

"I'm sorry. You startled me. Your hands, they're very..." Warmth moved up Willa's chest and into her cheeks. She stifled an overwhelming urge to shuffle her feet and stare at the ground.

"Just how new are those boots?"

"Very," she answered. She reached for the cream. "I think I'd better do my own feet."

"Suit yourself."

"Hmm." She had the feeling she didn't want to get that close, shouldn't get that close to this man, but the image of him rubbing her feet left her breathless. A peculiar tingling on the back of her neck had her turning to find the rapt attention of six curious budding teens. "Oh, boy," she moaned, then went back to work on her sore feet.

She had to get to the business at hand. Jeff was still wearing the jeans she'd slipped the camera in. The question was, had he found the pen and taken it out? And if he hadn't, how in the world was she going to get close enough to get it back from him?

She should tell him who she was and demand the pen. That would be the smart thing to do, the right thing to do, the *easiest* thing to do. It was exactly what Captain Ben Armstrong would do, but not what she would do.

Everyone would find out about Tracey's involvement with Jack Paulson soon enough. Bringing it all out into the open now would only fuel Jeff's instincts to protect the girl, and his actions could possibly jeopardize the case. No, she'd find a way to get the pen, then get out.

Willa glanced at the slight brunette across the fire

pit. *Haunted* was the word that came to mind. The poor thing looked haunted. If she only knew how lucky she was to be here tonight, among creatures and friends, and not with that monster, Jack.

Jeff dropped an armload of wood beside the fire pit and began to strategically pyramid the logs. He was quite handsome. Willa shook the thought right out of her head. He was a pastor who loved kids. Never had she run into anyone more out of her league than that. Even if his voice did shoot shivers down her spine, she couldn't allow herself the luxury of fantasizing about that or about him right now.

Right now, she had to find a way to get into his pants.

Chapter Three

Beyond the fire's flickering flames, Jeff watched curiously as Tracey stared at Willa. The girl's jaw was hardened and a slight scowl creased her brow. Tracey was overcome with anger. A feeling he knew only too well and had spent most of his life wresting to control. He rose and turned to their unexpected guest. "Willa, would you mind keeping an eye on the kids for a few minutes?"

"Me?" Willa's eyes widened in surprise. "Um. Sure. Okay, I guess I could do that." Skepticism lay thick in her voice. She stood up, looked around, then sat back down again.

Jeff smiled at the uncertainty playing across her face. Her eyes locked onto his. He didn't break the contact, but stood there baffled by the strange warmth spreading through him.

She blew back a stray, red curl that had fallen loose from its clip. "They won't wander off and get lost or anything, will they?"

"I don't think so," he murmured. "I mean, no, they won't. But if they do, they all have their whistles and they've been taught to hug a tree." He wondered what her hair would look like falling free around her shoulders.

"Hug a tree? Do you belong to some nature lover's organization or something?"

She couldn't be serious, Jeff thought. Certainly, she was teasing him. But he couldn't discern even the faintest flicker of amusement in her eyes. He stepped closer, close enough to smooth a smudge of dirt off her nose. He draped his whistle around her neck, then rested his hands on her shoulders. Something sparked in his fingertips. He almost pulled back, as a strong current quickened his pulse. He stared into the fathomless depths of her blue-green eyes. *Did she feel it, too?*

"If you get lost, find a tree, hug it, and blow the whistle." Caught on a lump in his throat, his voice sounded no louder than a whisper. He cleared it. "Don't keep wandering around or I won't be able to find you. It's basic wilderness rule 101."

Her mouth formed a perfect little O then widened into an embarrassed smile. "I knew that. Of course, I—" she clutched the whistle. "Thanks."

"Anytime," he said, feeling suddenly inane. Somehow this woman had him turned inside out. "God, grant me strength," he whispered and tried to clear her from his mind. But her faint vanilla scent lingered, toying with his imagination.

Suddenly, his resolve to stay free of romantic entanglements and concentrate on firmly establishing connections with the kids in his church wavered. But, he reminded himself, courting a woman, discovering if she had values and character traits that were in alignment with his took time. Time he needed to devote to his youth group. He'd once found a woman he thought could have been "the one," but he'd been wrong. And the distraction had cost him Dawn. He wouldn't make that mistake again—especially with Tracey. The troubled teenager would have his complete attention.

He turned to the girl. "Walk with me?"

She nodded, and keeping pace a few steps behind him, they left the camp and climbed deeper into the woods. Dusk came quickly here, bringing with it a multitude of insects, big and small. He swatted a flurry of mosquitoes out of his face, and tried to focus on the task at hand. "How are you feeling?"

"Fine." Her short, sweet, and clipped answer left him nothing to build on.

"Want to talk about it?"

"About what?"

About how you ended up on the strip poised to flush your life into L.A.'s almighty sewer, he thought. He shouldn't expect her to open up so quickly. The death of a parent was never easy, he knew all too well. First there was the grief, then the anger and sense of abandonment. It was hard for anyone to deal with, especially a thirteen-year-old girl.

"There's just something about her I don't trust."

Jeff looked at her, confused.

Tracey pulled at a branch as she passed it. "It's

clear that woman has never set foot outside her own backyard.''

''Oh,'' Jeff said, understanding. There was something to all those pouts and glares she had directed at Willa.

''She's a total fraud.''

''We don't know that. We shouldn't pass judgment.''

Tracey snorted. ''She's afraid of everything! She freaked at the sight of a snake. What had she expected, lying down in the grass? I can't wait to tell her to check herself for ticks.''

Jeff smothered a smile as he imagined the expression that would cross Willa's face. ''Let's give the lady a break, okay?''

''Why should I? Why is she even here?''

''What does it matter? Maybe she wanted to go hiking and took on a little more than she could handle.''

''Yeah, right. All by herself.''

Surprised by the venom in her voice, Jeff stopped and faced her. ''What's this really about?''

''I've seen her before,'' Tracey admitted. ''So have you.''

Nope. Jeff prided himself on remembering people and there was no way he could ever forget a woman like Willa. *Unfortunately.*

''You saw her this morning on the strip.''

A flicker of memory teased, but refused to sharpen into focus.

''Remember the blonde you thought you'd have to rescue?''

''The one who hadn't needed rescuing?'' How

could he forget? The way she'd handled that guy, kicking him with such intense force, he'd never seen anything like it. The two women had the same slight frame, but there was no way *that* woman, who took on two huge ruffians without batting a lash or breaking a nail, could be Willa. Jeff let out a shaky laugh. "Nah, no way."

"I got a good look at her in her apartment. It's her. It's Blondie. I swear it. Only her hair is different. And her clothes."

An illusive memory snapped into place; a tendril of curly red hair slipping out from under a blond wig to dance along a silky smooth jaw. Uneasiness twisted inside him. "What would she be doing here?" he thought aloud.

"What if she's come to take me back? What if Mr. Paulson sent her for me?"

The trembling in Tracey's voice caught Jeff by surprise. He took both her hands into his own. "Don't worry, Tracey. I would never let that happen. Believe me?" he asked when she didn't respond.

She nodded, but wouldn't look at him.

"I'm glad to hear you don't want to go back. I'd hate to have to face that man again myself."

"I don't. I swear. He was creepy. *Real* creepy."

"Are you willing to work with your mom to solve your problems at home?"

She fell into silence again and suddenly she looked so much younger than her thirteen years, so lost and alone.

"She's lost a lot, too. Give her a chance to figure out how to make it work."

"I don't think she can."

"Mothers aren't any more perfect than pastors."

She finally looked at him, a grim smile crossing her face. "Except for you. *You* are definitely perfect." Her tone dropped. "You came for me."

He slipped an arm around her shoulder and pulled her close. "I hope I'm always there when you need me, but you know God will always be there for you." He led her back down the trail, but she hesitated as the camp came into view. "Don't worry any more tonight about Jack Paulson or Willa," he said. "I don't know why she's here, but I swear I won't let anything happen to you."

Tears misted her large, brown eyes, darkening the doubt he saw lingering within. "Promise?" she asked, her voice sounding small and scared.

He cupped her chin and hoped the intensity of his gaze convinced her. "It's a solemn oath."

"I'm sorry I ran away."

"Life isn't always going to be easy, Tracey. Losing your dad is more than you should have to deal with. I know it isn't fair, and it isn't right. And, unfortunately, I don't have an easy answer as to why this horrible tragedy had to happen to your family. But put your faith in God. If you can face what He throws at you and grow from the challenges, you'll be a better and stronger person for it."

"You think?"

"No, I don't think." He smiled. "I know. You're a smart kid. If you start making smart decisions then everything will work out for you. The question is, do you believe it?"

She smiled. "I think so."

"Well, then, for the remainder of this trip let's work on you *knowing* so. Okay?"

"All right."

As they walked into the camp, Jeff couldn't help wondering if Tracey was right. Was Willa the bleached blonde who'd given him a back full of bruises? No wonder poor Tracey had been moping around. What could the woman possibly be doing here? For as sure as he knew there was a heaven in the sky, he knew Willa's arrival was no coincidence.

He saw her sitting before the fire, wiggling her toes in the warmth of the flames. She looked soft and sweet with her rust-colored curls coming to life in the fire's glow. Not in a million years would he have picked her as one of Jack Paulson's girls. She didn't look worn enough, nor were her edges hard or sharp enough. He remembered Dawn's wan face as it had been the last time he'd seen her alive. He pushed the image from his mind. Willa definitely didn't have the look of a girl who'd spent much time on the streets.

He'd always thought of himself as a good judge of people. Could he have been so wrong with this one? Willa turned and caught his stare, matching the intensity of his gaze with one of her own. She never backed down, this woman. Who are you, he wondered, and what are you doing here? One way or another, he'd find out.

He picked up his guitar, sat down in front of the fire, and strummed a few chords. One by one, the kids gathered around him. While he played "Jesus Loves Me," the kids sang along, their harmonious voices resonating through the mountain air. He closed his eyes and felt himself relax as his fingers moved over the strings. The instant his nerve endings tightened, he knew Willa had moved next to him. Even with his eyes shut, he could feel her presence.

He opened his eyes and saw her watching him with childlike wonder. She laughed, clapping in time. The gesture filled him with unexpected lightheartedness. He knew she was a walking, talking disaster. And yet, if anyone needed his help as much as Tracey, it was this woman. If only he knew what she was up to and what her connection was to Jack Paulson.

He watched her as they roasted hot dogs for dinner and toasted marshmallows for dessert. She ate and spent the evening talking quietly with the kids. She honestly seemed to be enjoying herself. Whatever her reason for being there, he was relieved to see she kept clear of Tracey. He'd wait until the others were asleep, he decided, then he and Lady Mysterious would have a talk.

Willa glanced behind her at the encroaching darkness, then inched closer to the fire. Even in the deepest alleys off Sunset Boulevard, she'd never experienced such complete darkness. She hugged her knees and stared into the crackling flames. The smell of wood smoke permeated her clothes, but she didn't mind. She was growing accustomed to the place, and she might even be enjoying herself, if it weren't for one tiny exception. She had to pee something fierce.

She peered again into the all-encompassing dark beyond the fire's glow. There wasn't anything out there now that wasn't there when the sun was up, she told herself firmly. Besides, if she didn't go soon her bladder would burst, and wouldn't that be amusing? She stood and reconnoitered the perimeter for the best direction to follow. She'd faced down L.A.'s worst scum; surely she could handle a few trees, bushes and darkness. Stop being a baby, she scolded herself. Tentatively, she took a step toward the trees behind Jeff's tent.

"Watch out for the mountain lions," Tracey called.

Willa hesitated, knowing full well she'd regret it.

"Lions and tigers and bears," Matt chimed in a high squeaky voice that cracked over the word *bears.*

"Oh, my!" the rest of the kids said in unison.

Willa turned.

"Lions and tigers and bears, oh my!"

Shocked, she stood there, staring at them. What a bunch of little beasts! Why would anyone want to go anywhere with six of them?

"All right. That's enough," Jeff scolded. "Give the poor lady some peace."

Willa cringed as she heard the restrained laughter in his voice.

Poor lady! She choked over his words. Is that really what they thought of her? Humiliation burned her to the core. The little predators had smelled her fear and moved in for the kill. "Very funny, you guys," she called, before slipping into the trees behind the tent. The sooner she got away from these people the better.

Lost in her thoughts, it wasn't long before she'd wandered too far from the fire's light and became disoriented in the darkness. Why hadn't she brought a flashlight? She couldn't see a thing. All she needed was to squat into a poison oak bush. Wouldn't that top off her day? Desk duty was looking better and better.

As soon as she'd finished, she made her way back in the direction she'd come, tucking in her shirt and zipping up her jeans as she went. Within a minute of trudging through the bushes, she heard the kids' voices and trotted back to the camp. The little brats were trying to spook her was all. She'd seen news reports of bears, torturing the metal of hapless cars while foraging for tortilla chips, but she couldn't recall anyone ever getting mauled by a mountain lion.

Don't let the kids get to you, she reminded herself. That would be a fatal mistake. Yet still…what if there were man-eating lions in the vicinity? She took one last look into the darkness before making her way back to the fire's glow. What she wouldn't give for Johnny's infrared goggles right now.

She retook her seat in front of Jeff's tent and caught him scrutinizing her again. Perhaps it was only the shifting light of the flames, but the expression on his face… She turned away, at once uncomfortable.

He stood, poking the fire from several angles, then sat down, positioning himself next to her. "Okay, guys. What do we do if we see a mountain lion?" he asked the kids.

Had she been that easy for him to read? No, stealth and duplicity were her most hard-won skills as an undercover cop. She'd never be able to do her job well without them. She wasn't transparent, of that she was confident. *Except perhaps by him?*

Maybe she wasn't deceiving him at all. Maybe he recognized her. The thought left her shaken. She didn't like the idea that *he* thought she was a hooker.

"Wave your arms above your head," Lisa yelled.

"Pick up a stick," Matt responded.

"Yeah, a big one," Kevin added.

"You're kidding, right?" Willa squeaked. They had to be kidding. "There aren't really mountain lions around here, are there?"

"Yep, along with wolves, coyotes, and bears." Jeff's large hand patted her knee, as if to say, "Don't worry, we'll take care of you." What did he think she was, a complete cream puff?

"Make yourself as large as possible," Charles answered.

"That's right," Jeff said.

Professional. She had to act professional. Don't let them smell fear. "Why don't you and I take turns keeping watch? I'll be happy to take the first shift." She couldn't imagine what he'd been thinking bringing six children up here alone. How responsible was that?

Matt laughed out loud, several others muffled snickers. She glared at them. Then again, they weren't exactly helpless babies, were they? Mountain lion bait, more like it.

"What for?" Jeff asked, though there was something about the tone of his voice.

Willa turned back to him. His lips contorted as he tried to smother a laugh. "For predators!" she exclaimed outraged. *Duh!*

Losing his battle, Jeff laughed long and hard, sending a rush of burning fury straight to her toes. ''Mountain lions are not interested in us. Just make sure all the dishes are cleaned and the food is sealed up, and the uh...*predators* will have no reason to come near here.''

Willa cringed. How had she gotten herself into this situation? Why hadn't she just booked a hotel room like the captain had suggested? Because she could find them in an hour, no problem, she silently mocked. *Dumb, dumb, dumb.*

''You can have my tent tonight.'' Jeff's voice cut through her torturous thoughts.

She looked up astonished. ''No, I couldn't do that.'' She clamped down on her lip, regretting the words the instant they slipped out of her mouth. Of course, she could. ''Where would you sleep?'' she asked softly, and berated herself for sounding like the wimp he believed her to be.

''Out here under the stars. I'll keep watch for the *predators.*''

She glared at him, certain he was laughing at her again. She could even see the laughter dancing in his eyes. She ached to punch him.

''Unless of course, you'd rather keep watch. I understand you're pretty good with your feet.''

''No, that's quite all right. You've seen one star, you've seen them all. But, thanks, I'll take you up on the tent offer.''

''My pleasure.'' He leaned close, his warm breath tickling her ear and sending shivers straight down her spine. ''Maybe in the morning you'll tell me exactly what you're doing here, Blondie.''

Dread sunk to the bottom of her stomach. *He knew.* What to do? What to do! "Um, if you don't mind, I think I'll go to sleep now." Direct avoidance, a woman's best tactic. She muffled an oversize yawn. "It's been quite a day. I'll see you in the morning." She got up, took her gear into the tent and zipped it up tight.

Only then did she allow herself to breathe. She'd get the evidence while he slept, then get out before dawn. With luck, she'd be halfway down the mountain before he even woke and realized she was gone. She arranged her sleeping bag then climbed in, squirming as she tried to find a softer bit of ground. What was under her anyhow, granite? Giving up on comfort, she laid back and stared into the darkness.

After a while, the noises died down, or maybe she just became used to them, and the kids went into their tents and all fell quiet. Taking a deep breath, she peeked through the tent's opening. True to his word, Jeff lay sprawled on the ground in front of her, staring up at the sky. How could anyone sleep where bugs and who knew what else could crawl all over you?

He wouldn't be out there if it weren't for you. She sighed. He was incredibly handsome, and kind, too. And the first man to set her heart racing in a very long time. And he thought she was a hooker. Oh well, what difference did it make? There wasn't a man alive who could see through to the real her. Not the cop—underpaid, underappreciated, and misunderstood—or the woman who'd obviously been alone for too long.

Maybe Ben was right; maybe she did need a life. Not that she'd had much luck with men in the past.

As soon as they got close, they were trying to change her, control her, mold her into their idea of the perfect woman. Well, perfect never looked good on her.

At last, his breathing evened. As quietly as possible, she opened the zipper and slipped out of the tent. In the dying glow of the firelight, she methodically searched around his sleeping bag for his jeans, but couldn't find them. Did he still have them on? She chewed her bottom lip. Of course he did; nothing about this trip was easy. Why should this be any different?

She grabbed the metal tongue of his sleeping bag and, inch by inch, slid the zipper down until the bag was opened to his waist. She glanced up at his face, her heart pounding so hard in her chest, she was afraid he might be able to hear it. She slipped her hand inside his bag and felt around. Tentatively, her fingers scraped across denim. Yep, he was definitely still wearing his jeans. She swallowed hard, then moved her hand around to the vicinity of his back pockets. He let out a soft groan.

Terror leaped into her chest.

His eyes opened.

She froze, unable to move, unable to breathe.

His eyes closed, then he rolled onto his side giving her easy access to the pen. She slipped it out of his pocket, and all but threw herself back into the tent. It wasn't until after she had herself zipped in tight and settled back down, her heart and breathing returning to normal, that she realized she'd forgotten to rezip his sleeping bag.

"Oh, man," she muttered. There was just no way,

no way, she was going back out there to do it again. He was an expert mountain man; he'd just have to take his chances with the lizards and snakes and all the other *predators* out there. Poor, poor man, Willa thought as she drifted to sleep.

The next morning, Willa woke to the mouthwatering scent of frying bacon and fresh mountain air. "Oh, no!" She sat straight up in her sleeping bag and bumped her head on the top of her tent. She'd overslept! Quickly, she dressed and reassembled her pack, careful to tuck the Pen Cam safely inside, then slipped out the tent.

Jeff stood with his back to her, watching the sunrise and drinking a cup of coffee. She spied the trail leading down the mountain, but was drawn back to the fire pit by the protesting groan of her stomach. The sight of his coffee and the smell of bacon sizzling over an open fire was more temptation than any mere woman could withstand.

She lugged her pack out of the tent's opening.

"Good morning," Jeff greeted. His sun-bleached hair, still tousled from sleep, hung boyishly over his brow.

She smiled. "Back at you."

"Hungry?"

"Ravenous."

"Coffee?"

"You really are too good to be true."

"That's what I've been told."

She quirked a brow, then took a large swallow from the cup he handed her. "Mmm. Coffee has never tasted so good. I never knew camping could be so civilized.''

''You've never been camping with me before.''

He caught her gaze and held it. Warmth rushed to her cheeks. ''No, I haven't.'' But that didn't mean she wouldn't want to. ''And it's been fab, really, but I need to get back to town.''

''So, you got what you came for then?''

Had he felt her searching for the pen? The thought made her squirm. ''Fresh air, a little exercise, yep—got it all right.''

''And that was *all* you are here for?''

His blue eyes probed as if she were a bug pinned under a magnifying glass. She flashed him a bright smile. ''I can't tell you how much I've appreciated your hospitality. If you hadn't found me and taken me in, well, I shudder to think what my night would have been like.''

''In other words, you have no intention of telling me anything, do you, Blondie?''

She was an ingrate, a total worm, and as she stared into the warmth of his eyes, she wanted to tell him. The urge was almost overwhelming. But suddenly, the explanation seemed too complicated. *I needed evidence that just happened to be hidden snugly in the back pocket of your jeans.* Yep, way too difficult. She couldn't start going soft now. Not for a handsome man with a nice pair of peepers.

''Maybe I'll look you up someday. We'll have coffee....''

''Yeah...sounds good, but I'm afraid I don't get down to your side of town often.''

Was that a slam? She stared him down. Okay, fine. He thought she was a hooker living in slimeville where his holiness had no intention of ever gracing. She could live with that. "How far are we exactly from the campground at the bottom of the trails?"

"About eight miles."

She gulped, scalding her throat on the hot liquid. "Eight?" No wonder her feet were a mess.

"Unfortunately, there's not one trail that will take you all the way down, since we jumped from trail to trail."

"I see," she said, at once thankful she'd overslept.

"I'll draw you a map."

"I guess it would be too much to hope for that you'll be heading my way?"

"Sorry, but we're going north another five miles to the Kern River where a boat is waiting for us. If you like river rafting, you're welcome to stay and join us."

An invitation for Blondie? Surprise arched her brows. She allowed herself to imagine floating down a peaceful river, her fingertips skimming the water's calm surface as she reclined against the side of the rubber raft. Hmm, sounded nice. And she wouldn't mind spending another day with a handsome pastor who kept her heart thumping and her nerves jumping. She'd never met a man who made her feel so alive. She sighed. Yes, it might be doable.

"I could use another adult to help row," he added before she could respond. "The person I had lined up got sick and bowed out."

Her fantasy faltered. "Row?" He didn't care about *her.* He just wanted another grown-up body. Too bad she could only manage ten minutes on the rowing machine at the gym. ‘‘Sorry,’’ she muttered. ‘‘It sounds fun, really, but I have to get back. Work, you know how it is.’’

He nodded and, for a minute, she fancied she read disappointment in his expression, but that couldn’t be. He thought she was a prostitute. The pastor and the prostitute, she could read the headlines now. Wouldn’t that give the captain a coronary? She wrapped a thick layer of gauze around her feet and shoved them into her boots.

‘‘I suppose it’s for the best. Your presence has upset Tracey.’’

‘‘Really? Why?’’

‘‘She recognized you from the strip.’’

Willa had already guessed that, but why did the girl consider her a threat? Unless she didn’t want her secret spilled. ‘‘I’m not here to bring harm to Tracey, or anyone else.’’

‘‘Then why are you here?’’

Willa bit her lip. ‘‘Like I said, just out for a hike. Imagine the odds of running into each other way out here?’’

‘‘Imagine,’’ he said dryly. He picked up a piece of paper and reached into his back pocket for the Pen Cam.

Oh, boy. Expectantly, she watched his brow crinkle into a frown before he dismissed the thought and went to his pack for another pen. ‘‘Tell Tracey she doesn’t have to worry about me,’’ she piped up. ‘‘And if she’s smart, she’ll stay away from Hollywood and Jack

Paulson. I know you believe in evil, and honey, he's as close to evil as I've ever seen."

"Then maybe you should stay away from him, too."

"That's the plan."

"Here." He handed her a crude map that she couldn't make heads or tails of.

"Thanks," she said and hesitated, a little surprised by her reluctance to leave. Was it the trek down the mountain, or the thought of leaving him? "Maybe I'll see you around back in L.A.?"

"Doubt it. Like I said, I don't spend a lot of time on your side of town."

"Right. Yeah, I suppose you wouldn't. It was great to meet you, Jeff." She offered her hand. Her smile faltered as the warmth of his touch trapped the breath in her throat. Yep, it was definitely the thought of leaving him. What a hunk. She turned and headed down the trail, refusing to glance over her shoulder for one last look.

She could do this, she told herself as the forest enveloped her. She had an excellent sense of direction. Everyone had always said so. She'd never once gotten lost in L.A., and with all those freeways that was quite an accomplishment. A few measly trails wouldn't confuse her. All she had to do was keep heading downhill. She trotted for a minute, pretending it was her morning run, until a heavy tightness banded her chest. Must be the altitude.

Stopping to catch her breath, she dug into her pack for her compass and cell phone. She'd call Ben and let him know she had the evidence and would be home by dinner. She pushed the power button, then waited for the familiar writing to appear across the screen. No reception, nothing.

"Man," she grumbled. "How do people function out here?" In disgust, she dropped the phone in her bag and studied her compass. Northwest. Great. What did that mean? Which direction had she left her car? *At the bottom of the hill, dummy.* She shoved the compass back in her pack and continued down the trail. All the trails had to lead to the same place, so if she just stayed on this one, she'd get there. Eventually.

After another twenty minutes, her feet began to sting. After forty, they were screaming for mercy. She found a big rock, sat on it, and pulled off her boots. "Eight miles," she grumbled. Why hadn't she just camped out at the bottom of the hill and waited for them to come down? Why was she always in such a hurry to get herself into these situations?

Because she was always in a hurry to prove herself, to be the one to bring in the goods, never mind what was sensible. *Sensible* described Captain Ben, not her. That's why he was the captain and not a street grunt. She shook the distasteful thought out of her head, and dug into her pack for something to eat. She munched dry granola and cursed herself for not sticking around to eat Jeff's breakfast. "I bet they even had bagels," she said to the chipmunk who'd perched in front of her eyeing the granola.

What kind of man took six kids out into the wilderness and brought along makings for a bacon-and-eggs breakfast? A pretty wonderful one, she thought. And the way he played the guitar, all their voices joined in unison, singing from the heart without pause or embarrassment—she'd never experienced anything like that. It was truly wonderful. *He* was truly wonderful. A very special man. Not the kind of man who'd be interested in a streetwise cop from the wrong side of town, that's for sure.

If he was so special, she thought irritably, then how could he let her leave knowing she had to walk eight miles in the forest without a clue where she was going? What kind of special man did that?

Footsteps crunched the trail rocks behind her. Her heart soared. "Yes! Thank you!" She stood and turned, unable to quench the wide smile covering her face. "I knew you wouldn't leave me to suffer—" Her words caught in her throat as a huge bear lumbered toward her.

Chapter Four

Willa's knees weakened, threatening to buckle. She screamed. The sound ripping from her echoed through the mountain air. Turning, she tore off barefoot down the trail afraid to stop or look back until her insides burned and she was gasping for breath.

Finally, she stopped and bent down, swinging her head between her knees and looked back at the trail behind her. She was alone. No giant grizzly in sight. "Thank, God," she huffed and took a few more steps before she realized she didn't have her pack. *She had to go back!* The ridiculous thought quickened her heart. She tried to catch her breath, but couldn't. She was hyperventilating!

She limped another few steps, wincing as a sharp stone bit into her toe. She couldn't walk eight miles through the woods barefoot, and she couldn't go back without that Pen Cam.

"Argh!" she yelled. It didn't matter if Godzilla

himself waited at the top of the trail; she had to go back for that blasted pen!

Willa winced at her dumb luck with every torturous step back up the trail. Boy, she'd run far. She took every turn slowly, peeking around the bend, not sure where the hairy beast would show up next. Maybe he realized his breakfast had run off and moved on to greener pastures.

Then again, maybe not.

She rounded the next turn and stopped, outrage eclipsing all other emotions. Her pack, trampled and torn, laid ripped open. Packaged remains of food items littered the ground. The bear sat amidst the ruins working her tube of toothpaste and smacking his minty paste-covered tongue. Was he actually smiling? And was that her deodorant clumped all over his chest?

"You beast! Why don't you go up the hill? You can have bacon and eggs up there. And bagels with cream cheese, probably even strawberry cream cheese!"

The bear turned a lazy stare in her direction and continued to lap the tube.

"You don't look so big and scary. In fact, you look pretty ridiculous with my underwear on your head."

The bear yawned.

"Go find yourself a nice cave and take a nap. Take the toothpaste with you. It's all yours." She gave him a shooing gesture.

The bear dropped the tube, swatted one of her boots, then returned his attention to her pack.

"Oh, no you don't!" Wasn't she supposed to act big around bears? Or was that mountain lions? Whichever, did it really matter? Desperation revving confidence, Willa swooped her arms up and down in imitation of a giant pterodactyl and made deep whooping noises while moving closer to the bear.

The dumb beast turned and looked at her, grunted, then gave her a view of his backside before pawing through her pack again.

"Oh, great. A tough audience." What to do? "Hai yah!" she yelled and thrust out an arm at him, palm forward, fingers curled.

No response.

Next she brought up a leg, kicking the air in front of the bear in quick rapid thrusts. "Whaaa chai!" she shouted at the top of her lungs, throwing out every move she could remember from her Tae Boxing class.

If a bear could laugh, he was laughing at her now. She could see it in his dirty-brown eyes. "Oh!" she screamed in frustration and jumped up and down in a tantrum only a two-year-old could appreciate. "Would you just get out of here and leave me alone?" She picked up a stick and threw it, hitting him square in the head. "Bull's-eye!"

Standing on hind legs and reaching for the sky, the bear bellowed. His growl, rumbling through the forest, struck terror into Willa's heart. Eyes popping, she screamed, "I'm sorry! Really! I didn't mean it."

The bear growled louder.

In a panic, she ran past him as fast as she could, up the trail, and rammed straight into Jeff, knocking him flat to the ground and falling on top of him.

His groan rivaled the bear's growl. "Is this going to be a daily thing?"

''Hurry,'' she insisted. ''Before he eats us.''

''I think he's already had breakfast.''

Looking over her shoulder, Willa saw the beast, her toothpaste smeared in his fur, give them a cursory glance then plod off down the trail and disappear into the woods. She expelled a relieved sigh and dropped her head onto Jeff's chest. The steady rhythm of his heartbeat quieted her racing nerves. Slowly, her breathing returned to normal.

''You came back for me?'' she squeaked, suddenly aware of his body beneath hers—strong and warm.

''Matt wouldn't leave without you. Said you'd never make it back down the hill alone.''

''Remind me to thank him,'' she muttered. She should get off him, knew it was the decent thing to do. She just couldn't seem to make herself do it.

''You can do that yourself.''

''I can?'' She looked up into his face. His lips mere inches from hers looked so soft, so inviting.

''When I take you back to camp.''

His words registered through the hazy fog of her thoughts. She sat up, quickly. ''Back to camp? I can't go back to camp! I have to get back to my Jeep. Back to L.A.''

''And I have to get back to my kids. I've left them alone long enough. So, you have a choice. You can pick up what's left of your stuff and continue the rest of the way on your own, or you can come back to camp with me and spend the next two days in God's country, floating down a river, communing with nature, and relaxing.''

''Oh,'' she moaned.

''It's up to you.'' He held both hands out, moving them up and down, measuring. ''Work, vacation? Work, vacation?''

''Some vacation,'' she muttered.

He arched a brow.

''Oh, all right, you have me. What choice do I really have? You and I both know I'd never make it down to my Jeep alone.''

''You might, eventually.''

''Yeah, like in a hundred years.''

Twenty minutes later they crested the hill and came upon the camp. The kids had everything packed and ready to go. ''How'd we get here so fast?'' Willa asked amazed.

''We took the most direct route.''

''What's that supposed to mean?''

''That, my dear, means that you were walking in circles.''

''Hey, are you all right?'' Matt asked, running to meet them. ''We heard a scream.''

''We're fine,'' Jeff answered. ''Our friend here had a run-in with a bear.''

''Wow,'' Matt said, awed.

''Did she drop into a dead faint?'' Tracey asked with an innocent smile. Willa was quickly losing her patience with the child.

''Quite the opposite. You should have seen her fancy moves. Gave that bear a thing or two.''

Willa stared at him in astonishment. ''You saw?''

Jeff crouched down, extended an arm, and yelled ''Whaaa chai,'' kicking out his arms and legs in rapid comedic succession. ''The bear never had a chance.''

And neither did she.

The kids erupted into fits of laughter—two rolling on the ground, clutching their stomachs.

Embarrassment burned Willa's face. Though, she couldn't help laughing with them. In fact, she laughed so hard tears leaked out the corners of her eyes. "Stop, please," she begged.

"Well gang, it looks like we have a new addition on our adventure."

"Yeah," Matt whooped. The other kids joined in. Everyone, Willa noticed, except for Tracey.

With Willa's pack held together with duct tape and her feet rebandaged, they set out toward the river. Gradually, she fell behind the troop, listening to the girls' chatter, watching the boys' roughhouse each other, and admiring the easy manner in which Jeff dealt with them all.

"Poison oak," Lisa yelled and skirted the green bush that looked to Willa like every other bush in the forest. How could she tell them apart? She walked around the bush, careful not to brush against the leaves, or even breathe until she was safely past. Soon, they made their way through a grove of immense trees towering toward the sky.

"Let's take a break here," Jeff announced, and sat at the base of one of the massive trunks.

Willa stopped and stared. "These are incredible," she murmured.

"They're giant sequoias," Jeff said. "The largest trees to inhabit the earth."

Willa had never seen trees so big. She touched the

soft stringy red bark, then walked around the expanse of the trunk.

"How old is it?"

"Some of these date back to before Jesus walked the earth."

"Amazing."

"Only God could make something this beautiful," he said softly, his fingertip tracing the grooves in the bark.

"Perhaps you're right. I've never seen anything like them." They stood silent for a moment, paying homage to one of Mother Nature's finest accomplishments.

"You look good against them."

Something in his voice tickled Willa's spine. She turned to him.

"Your hair. It's the same color as the bark."

"Oh. Um…thanks." Awareness of how close he was grew within her, constricting her breath.

"You should get out of the city more, roughing it looks good on you."

She grimaced at the thought of how she looked when he first saw her on the strip. "What makes you think I don't? Get out more."

His knowing smile prickled her ire.

He knew nothing about her, and yet, at moments like this, was there anything he didn't know? Well, yes. He didn't know she was a cop—that was for sure. The man thought she was a hooker. How off base was that, considering how extremely unlimited her experiences with men were? Most men were either intimidated or disgusted by her commitment to the streets. Not one had stuck around long enough to discover who she really was, and why she was so committed to taking down Jack Paulson. The last had just spouted words like *vengeance* and *obsession,* but he really hadn't had a clue. It was about so much more than that; it was about taking back her life.

Nope, Jeff didn't know a thing about her.

They joined the others in the deep shadows of the mammoth trees. Jeff handed her a sandwich. "I made these this morning."

"How'd you know I'd be along?"

"An educated guess."

She frowned. She hoped she wasn't becoming predictable.

"Monica, will you say grace?"

Willa paused with her sandwich halfway to her mouth.

A small girl with yellow hair and a slew of freckles across her nose bent her head and squinted shut her eyes. Willa couldn't help but smile at her; such innocence was irresistible.

"Dear God, thank you for this food and this wonderful land with all the beautiful trees and animals. Please bless our families and take special care of our new friend, Willa, that she doesn't get eaten by a mountain lion or a bear. That she doesn't drown in the river, or fall off a cliff, or get bitten by a snake, since she isn't used to the wilderness. Amen."

"Amen," everyone said in unison with laughter glinting in their sweet, young eyes.

And here she was thinking such nice thoughts about the child.

''Thank you,'' Willa responded, and was rewarded with a flurry of giggles and six toothy grins.

''I think they like you,'' Jeff volunteered, and handed her a water bottle.

''Gee, aren't I lucky?''

''Believe me, you are. You don't know how fun camping can be with six prepubescent teens who don't like you.''

Willa shuddered at the thought. ''I can only imagine. Have you done this long? I mean, camping with kids.''

''This is our second annual trip. It's a great way for me to get to know the kids better—for us to bond with each other. At their age, it's critical they have someone to talk to who will listen to them. Someone who won't judge no matter what they've done.''

''Like Tracey,'' Willa whispered, and glanced at the girl who was deep in conversation with Monica and Lisa.

''Exactly like Tracey. Her dad died last year. Since then, her mom's been too wrapped up in functioning alone to realize how much Tracey's needed her. Running away was a cry for help.''

''She's very lucky to have you.''

A self-conscious smile lifted the corners of his lips and she had to catch her breath again.

''Thanks, ma'am,'' he said with a bow.

''You're welcome. You're really good with them. How'd you learn to do that?''

He smiled. ''Did you go to church when you were a kid?''

She shook her head. ''My parents didn't have much time for religion.''

He gave her a knowing nod. ''Unfortunately, that's the case for a lot of parents out there. Asking God into your life is a big commitment, but the best one a person can make.''

She nodded, not knowing how to respond. She didn't see how going to church on Sundays could possibly improve her life.

''Anyhow, I spent a lot of time in church youth groups growing up. Becoming a youth minister was a natural progression for me. It's easy to know how to be with the kids, because I've always been with them. The key is to never forget what it felt like to be one.''

''Hey, you two, let's get a move on,'' Matt called from the trail.

''You're the boss, lead on,'' Jeff yelled.

As they continued through the woods, Willa mulled over his words. She had to admit she didn't remember what it had felt like to be thirteen. She didn't want to remember; she didn't want to go back to that time of overwhelming grief, loneliness, and pain.

At last she caught glimpses of the river peeking through the trees. As they approached, sunlight glinted off clear sparkling water. Hundreds of tiny fish swam around the rocks at her feet. She stuck her hands in the water to catch one of the slippery little fish, but they were too quick for her. Laughing, she gave up, scooped the water in both hands, and splashed it across her face.

She felt Jeff watching her, looked up and gave him a smile. How different would her life have turned out if she'd found someone like him back when her dad had died? Would she have known what it felt like to sleep under the stars and cleanse her face with pure mountain river water? If she had, would she now be able to trust another person with her hopes, her secrets, her dreams? Would she be able to let another person close to her?

A moment of sadness hit her for all she'd lost as a child. All that Jack Paulson had stolen from her when he'd killed her dad. If only Ben had been able to nail him then; if only someone could have done something. How different would her life have been? Maybe she would have even grown into the type of person who would have a chance with someone like Jeff—someone undamaged and happy, someone with a future beyond the darkness of the streets.

"There's the boat," Matt called.

Willa shook off the thoughts. She'd managed fine then, and she was managing just fine now. *Alone.*

Upriver, a rubber raft large enough to fit the eight of them drifted with the current, pulling against its tether.

"There are only seven oars," Monica yelled.

"Too bad. Looks like there isn't one for me," Willa joked.

"Don't worry. I'll make sure you get a turn. We've got to keep up your strength in case we run across any more bears."

He was laughing at her again. "You really are too charming for words."

"I wouldn't want you to miss out on all the fun."

"Nope, that would be a tragedy," Willa said.

''Absolutely.''

''How did the boat get here?''

''I have a friend who brings it up for me,'' Jeff replied. ''When we reach the bottom of the river he'll pick us up and drive us back to our van. And you to your Jeep.''

That was the best news she'd heard all day. ''When will we reach the rendezvous point?''

''Rendezvous point?'' he asked, his head cocked sideways.

She shrugged.

''Day after tomorrow.''

''Any way to speed that up?''

''No, and we don't have any way of contacting him.''

''What if one of the kids got hurt? Fell off a cliff or something,'' she said with a pointed look at Monica.

''Then I'd radio a ranger for help.''

''Can you radio a ranger to come get me and take me back to my Jeep?''

''No.''

''Why not?'' she asked, her tone seriously approaching a whine.

''What if someone needed him and he wasn't able to help because he was stuck playing taxi to a spoiled city girl who couldn't last two days in the wilderness?''

''I am not a spoiled city girl!''

''I can tell by those nails.''

Willa studied her perfectly polished red nails. ''These are part of my—''

Jeff quirked a brow.

Willa groaned. She'd almost blown it again. What was wrong with her? ''Hey, don't you worry about me. I can keep up with all you die-hard campers, just watch.''

''If that's the case, why couldn't you find your way down the mountain?'' The venom in Tracey's words caught Willa off guard. Jeff had said Tracey was afraid of her, but this...perhaps it was time to set the child straight.

''I'm not here to cause you or anyone else any problems.''

The girl glared at her.

''I mean it, Tracey.'' Great, now she sounded just like her mother used to.

''Come on, let's go,'' Matt insisted.

They climbed into the boat and paddled in unison, moving quickly down the river. Willa hated to admit it, but she was having fun. The clean air on her face, the magnificent trees, the endless blue sky, she loved it all. She watched Jeff paddling in front of her, his wide shoulders swaying in rhythm as his arms effortlessly pushed the oar against the water. She steadied herself, matching his pace, focusing on his back muscles as they rippled beneath his shirt. Yep, the view out here was beyond words.

''So, Willa, where do you live?'' Matt asked from behind her.

''L.A.''

''What do you do?''

''Not much.''

She turned to him. ''What do you do?''

''Not much,'' he challenged.

She smiled. ''What do you want to do when you grow up?''

''I'm going to be an animator,'' Matt responded.

''Wow, sounds great. I can't draw to save my life.''

''It's not hard, I'll give you a few pointers tonight around the fire, if you'd like.''

''Sure, sounds fun.'' Willa smiled.

Kevin swung his oar and doused Matt with a face full of water. ''Isn't she a little old for you, Matty boy?''

''Hey,'' Matt protested, and retaliated with the same. The boat rocked precariously, and in the scuffle, they tromped all over Willa's pack, spilling some of its contents.

''Hey, you guys, calm down,'' she shouted, and struggled to secure everything back in the pack. Covertly, she moved her hand over the Pen Cam making sure it was still in its place.

Jeff threw her the roll of duct tape. She peeled off long strips, and wrapped them around the pack, holding its ripped sides together.

''Here, let me help,'' Charles stated, and took the roll.

''Thanks, Charles.''

''Sorry, Willa,'' Matt said.

''It's fine. No reason to be sorry.''

''What about the rest of you?'' Jeff asked. ''What do you all want to be when you have to leave the bosom of your parents' home and embrace the cold, cruel world?''

''Oh, man,'' Charles protested. ''That was bad.''

When no one spoke up, Jeff continued, "How about you, Tracey?"

She glared at Willa. "I think I'll be a hooker down on the strip and make so much money I'll never have to answer to anyone again. I'll be an independent woman and never have to work, just like my friend here, Blondie."

Willa sat stunned amidst the gasps in the boat.

"Get out," Kevin exclaimed.

"Yeah, as if," Matt responded.

"Come on, Blondie. Admit it," Tracey challenged.

"Tracey, I'm not a hooker."

"You're a liar. You've done nothing but lie since you got here."

Willa cringed. What could she say? The girl had a point. Concern filled Jeff's face. She could only imagine what was racing through his mind. How would all those uptight Pasadena parishioners react when they discover Pastor Jeff invited a hooker along on their young'uns camping trip? Yep, she'd be concerned, too.

She could jump overboard and make her way downriver along the water's edge. She glanced into the trees lining the shore. But then what would she do once the sun went down? Cuddle up next to a mountain lion to stay warm? Dumb idea. Besides, if she jumped into the water with this monolithic pack, she'd drown for sure. The thing was the equivalent of cement shoes.

"Well?" Tracey demanded.

"Tracey, that's enough," Jeff ordered, and placed a hand on her shoulder.

He might be able to stop her words, but he couldn't

do anything about what they all must be thinking. "Listen, you guys," Willa started. "I'd like to tell you a story about a brave man, a good man—the best dad anyone could ever have, and he was mine."

Tracey feigned a bored expression and looked away.

"He was shot dead in an alley when I was twelve. Murdered. Just like that—" she snapped her fingers "—he was gone. I know you suffered a devastating loss, too, Tracey."

Tracey's stare burned anger and defiance. "Don't pretend you know anything about me."

"You're right. I don't know anything about you and your life, but for me, I couldn't get over it. I have devoted every second of the last fifteen years devising a way to make his killer pay. That's what *I* was doing down on the strip."

"Cool," Matt muttered.

"Awesome," Charles agreed.

Willa rolled her eyes in disgust. It wasn't cool or awesome; it was war. And she needed to get back to the battlefield and stop wasting her time with a bunch of kids who thought she was some kind of crusader. They chattered excitedly among themselves about good guys and bad guys, and their favorite TV shows.

Not Tracey; she sat in a cloud of resentment. And not Jeff; his look was quiet and speculative. She knew her explanation had appeased the kids, but it still hadn't explained how she coincidentally ended up in his lap...so to speak. Willa dropped a foot over her pack and pulled it closer to her. It wouldn't do to have the evidence wind up in the river.

"The Bible says to forgive your enemies. The Lord

will judge the world in righteousness and the peoples with equity,'' Monica said, softly.

''I wish I was a strong enough person to do that, Monica. But I'm not. I don't believe in divine justice. I don't believe God was there with my father the night he was mercilessly gunned down, and I don't believe He's been with me since.''

Monica and the others' wide-eyed stares were her first clue that perhaps she'd come on a little too strong. She gently patted the girl's shoulder. ''I only hope God will always be there for you, and that your faith will remain as strong and unwavering as it is today.''

''And I hope you will find yours again.''

Willa smiled wanly, and was surprised to find her eyes misting. Quickly, she turned away. No, God had abandoned her long ago. Like Santa Claus, He was a dream of happiness and hope that was best left to the youth.

Chapter Five

Jeff sat stunned. Of course. Why hadn't he figured it out sooner? Willa was a cop. That's why he was having such a hard time getting a handle on her. She was a cop whose sole focus boiled down to vengeance for her father's death. She'd turned her back on God just when she'd needed Him the most.

Sadness besieged him. Here was a woman who made him laugh and had him constantly wondering what she would say and do next. She was strong and courageous and perfectly capable of taking care of herself. But he didn't think he'd ever run across anyone who needed his help and God's love more.

"Let's stop up ahead at the clearing beyond that granite slab. We'll make camp there for the night," he announced. They tethered the boat to the shore, then unloaded their supplies. "Head out in pairs to gather wood. Remember to watch for snakes."

"Yeah, Lisa. Watch out for snakes," Kevin teased.

"Stuff it, Kevin."

"Oh, Lisa is getting mad," he bantered.

They scampered off into the woods, their voices becoming faint echoes.

Once they were alone, Jeff turned to Willa before she could disappear, too. "Are you a cop?"

She bit her lip, then seeming to make up her mind, looked him square in the eye. "Yes."

"And you're after Jack Paulson?"

"That's the plan."

"So, what's that have to do with us? Why are you here?"

Her mouth opened, ready to spill some preplanned story, but he stepped forward, placing his hands on her shoulders, his face inches from hers. "The truth."

Uncertainty played across her expression.

"Please."

Willa bent down, dug into her pack and pulled out a pen. "I came for this."

Jeff stared at it. "A pen?"

"I slipped it into your pocket after I knocked you down on the sidewalk yesterday morning."

Jeff rubbed his shoulder at the memory.

"Inside is a video recording of Jack enticing Tracey to stay and work for him. With this evidence, we can nail him for harboring a runaway at the least, and child prostitution at the worst."

The full implication of her words sunk in. This would hit the news. Everyone would know what Tracey had done. "I don't want Tracey's life ruined. I don't want her to have to testify."

Willa's eyes hardened.

"She doesn't need the people in her life to know

what she's done, the mistakes she's made...it could set her back."

"I realize that, Jeff. But we have to do whatever it takes to get a conviction. She might be embarrassed, but nothing happened. You got to her in time."

Her words hung suspended between them. Had he? He'd made that mistake once before, thinking he'd reached Dawn in time, but he'd been wrong. "I'm sorry, but I can't take that chance. Not with Tracey. She's too young and too vulnerable."

"Even if it means Paulson walks?"

He wanted Jack Paulson put away as badly as she did, and all those like him who preyed on children. "Let's hope you're a good enough cop that you'll be able to lock him up without her."

Her chin lifted, her gaze steady as she met his challenge.

"I'm inclined to think you'll be able to do just that," he added.

"Thanks for the vote of confidence, but with this case, I need all the help I can get."

"Help with what?" Charles asked, appearing on the path behind them.

"Gathering wood for a fire," Jeff answered.

Willa smiled sweetly at the boy and, once again, Jeff was struck by the different facets to her—tough yet vulnerable, kind yet there was an unwavering layer of defense that refused to reveal her soft spot.

After a few moments, Charles trotted off happy to have a job. Willa touched Jeff's arm. "I know why you're protecting Tracey."

Could she?

''I admire the way you're helping her cope with her loss. It's wonderful.''

''Yes, that's part of it. But it's not wonderful. It's just what I do. Who I am. These kids are on the brink, old enough that the decisions they make now will shape their entire futures, yet young enough to not always use sound judgment.''

She nodded. ''Like I said on the boat, I lost my dad when I was Tracey's age. I know what she's feeling, the abandonment and the fear of being alone.'' She sat on a large boulder.

''He was a police officer, too?''

''The best. What about you, how did you become a youth minister?''

''I guess you could say I followed in my father's footsteps, too. He's the head pastor at the Pasadena Church.''

''All in the family, huh?''

''My father wouldn't have had it any other way.'' A bubble of resentment expanded inside him. He pushed it back down. ''But all the same, I'm pleased with the work that I do, and the impact I'm able to have on the children. Reminding them that God is always there for them, guiding them, if they'd only quiet their hearts and listen.''

''It's a nice sentiment.''

He could see the shutters dropping over her eyes. ''But…''

''But it doesn't work for me. I'm afraid God has never been there for me, and most likely never will.''

Sadness swept through him at her words. ''I think

God's been trying to reach you for a long time, but you haven't slowed down enough to listen."

Her smirk didn't deter him.

"He can't reach you if you won't let Him."

"Sorry, Reverend, but I'm too old and jaded for your special type of magic. I've seen too many bad things, too much horror to believe if there was God, he'd let so many good people be hurt."

"Yes, but—"

"Please don't tell me that God works in mysterious ways because I don't have any more patience for that than I do for the Jack Paulsons in the world."

Her bitterness shouldn't have surprised him. She'd allowed herself to become too pessimistic, too resentful from spending too much time on the streets with people who were lost—people who needed help the most. He remembered their struggle very well from his days at the Sun Valley parish.

He hoped he'd made life a little easier for some of them. Just like he hoped he could help Willa. She deserved to understand that God loved her and was with her all the time. She deserved peace of mind. He just hoped she would do right by Traccy, because as much as Willa needed him, Tracey needed him more.

"Jeff! Willa!"

They heard the panicky voice seconds before the trampling of the underbrush. Matt broke into the clearing, red-faced and winded.

With one look at Matt's scared face, fear seized Jeff's heart. "What is it?"

"It's Tracey. She's—" Matt bent over, trying to catch his breath.

Jeff swallowed the tennis-ball-size lump in his throat.

"—she's been taken."

"What do you mean, 'taken?'" Jeff stood dumbstruck. "There isn't anyone around here for miles."

"Paulson," Willa choked under her breath. She grabbed the boy's arm. "Matt, tell us exactly what you saw."

"I climbed up onto the top of a huge rock to get a better view for my sketches." He unconsciously waved the sketchpad still clutched in his hand. "I saw Tracey on the path below me, following one man and being pushed from behind by another. She looked scared. Real scared."

"What did these men look like? Can you describe them for me?"

"Big. Definitely big. Wearing jeans. Yeah, blue jeans."

Willa caught Jeff's eye and easily read the questions dwelling there, since she had the same fears ripping at her insides. Her cover was blown and Paulson was cleaning up the trail that led to him. If she didn't get Tracey back—and soon—the girl wouldn't live long enough to testify against him. Paulson knew what he was doing. An accident in the woods would be hard to trace.

She turned to Jeff. "Radio for help, use my name and have the local authorities update Captain Ben Armstrong of the L.A. police department. Gather the kids here, and let no one out alone. No one! Matt, show me the trail."

''That way,'' he said, pointing to the path that led along the river.

Jeff placed a hand on her shoulder. ''How do you plan on stopping them? They must have weapons. You can't go out there alone. Let me help you.''

''No way. You have to protect the children.''

Concern filled his eyes. She softened her tone and grabbed his hand, giving it a gentle squeeze. ''Don't worry about me, okay? I'm used to working alone. And I'm not entirely without a weapon.'' She shook out her right foot. ''These feet are mighty powerful.''

''How could I have forgotten?'' he said dryly.

She could see she hadn't convinced him. ''Don't forget, Carlos didn't get everything he wanted. They'll be back for the evidence. Watch the kids.'' She tucked the Pen Cam into her back pocket. ''See if the rangers can get up here, pronto. Have the boat ready, just in case. We can't stay here tonight. God only knows how they managed to track us down.''

Before he could protest any further, she was off and running.

''I'll be back before you know it. With Tracey!'' she called, and disappeared down the path.

He was right, Willa thought as she ran out of his sight. This wasn't something she could handle on her own. She didn't know the first thing about tracking in the wilderness, and they could be anywhere by now, even though they couldn't have had more than a five-minute head start on her. If she ran, perhaps she could catch up with them. But then what?

They'd be armed. There were two of them, she didn't have her gun and, let's face it, Carlos wasn't playing with a full deck. The man was a raving lunatic and that gave him an edge she didn't have. Where was her pal Mr. Grizzly now? "I could use some divine intervention here, God!" she called and rounded the next bend without even slowing.

After about ten minutes of full out sprinting, she heard something, but was breathing too loudly to be sure. Reluctantly, she stopped and tried to still her heaving chest.

"What do you want from me?" Tracey's voice rang through the trees.

Willa let out a sigh of relief. She was close. She trotted to the next bend and rounded it just in time to see the trio weaving through the trees at the far end of the path. Tracey's terrified expression as Carlos snarled at her and shoved her forward wrenched something inside her, filling her with cold determination.

For the next twenty minutes, Willa trailed behind them as closely as she dared. It wouldn't do to be discovered before she had a plan. She glanced at the sky, and knew from the night before that darkness fell quickly. They had less than an hour, and it didn't appear as though Carlos planned to set up camp.

Jeff pulled out his radio and hailed the ranger station, but he knew as far up as they were, reaching them would take time and by then it would be dark. And conducting a search after dark wasn't easy. He promised Tracey he'd be there for her, that he wouldn't let the bad guys win. How could this have happened? Fear ate away at him, muddling his thoughts, leaving him confused and opening the door to his frustration and anger. He slammed shut the door. *Please God, please let her be safe. Let Willa find Tracey and lead them back to safety.*

Matt returned with the other four kids in tow. The scared look on his face reminded Jeff just how young and vulnerable all the kids were.

"Hey, what's up?" Kevin asked.

"Yeah, Matt made it sound like some kind of an emergency," Monica added.

Jeff looked into their expectant faces and didn't know what to say, or how much. He hadn't even figured out what they should do.

"Tracey's in trouble," Matt said, solving Jeff's dilemma. Matt already knew about Carlos. The rest would have to know, too.

"What kind of trouble?" Kevin demanded.

"And where's Willa?" Charles asked. "Is she in trouble, too?"

"Was it a bear or a snake?" Lisa looked around the camp, her eyes searching the bushes.

"It wasn't a bear or a snake," Jeff said. "Sit down. All of you."

They did as he asked, sitting on boulders, logs and their packs. Once he had their attention, he explained the best way he knew how.

"Some men have taken Tracey?" Monica asked with a quaver in her tone. "How could that have happened way out here?"

"What are they going to do to her? What do they want?" Lisa whined, her big eyes round and scared.

"All right, calm down." Jeff's head was beginning to spin. "Willa is a police officer working for the Los

Angeles Police Department. She is familiar with the men who took Tracey. She's gone after them and she'll bring Tracey back.'' He hoped. But even as he said the words, he knew it was highly improbable, if not downright impossible.

He worried for her, worried what those men were capable of. Dawn's battered face entered his mind. His fists clenched at his sides. He couldn't go through that again, he just couldn't.

''Yeah, right,'' Kevin sneered. ''That woman couldn't even make her way back down the mountain and we're supposed to believe she'll be able to find her way back here to us?''

You better believe she will, Jeff thought. *She has to.*

''She just happens to stumble onto us,'' Kevin continued, his fists bunched at his sides. ''And two men she just happens to know come by and kidnap Tracey. Like I believe that! I say we go after them.''

''All right, Kevin. That's enough. You're not helping the situation,'' Jeff scolded, but he shared Kevin's frustration. They just couldn't sit there and hope Willa could bring down two men in the wilderness alone, and find her way back to them.

Kevin stomped back and forth in front of Jeff, his face flushed and angry. ''You aren't really going to leave Tracey's rescue up to this so-called lady cop, are you? I mean, come on, man! There's no way she can get Tracey away from two guys on her own.''

''Big guys. And she's not armed, either,'' Matt stated matter-of-factly.

"Oh, great. What are we waiting for? Let's go get Tracey!" Kevin grabbed his pack.

"Yeah," Matt agreed, and followed suit.

"No way, we're staying right here," Jeff insisted, and stood before the boys, blocking their way. Luckily, he still towered over them.

"Chicken!" Kevin called.

"Gobble, gobble," Matt added.

"Knock it off," Monica snapped.

"All right, that's enough." Jeff was losing control fast. Not only of them, but of himself. "Of course I want to go after Tracey. But I can't risk the rest of you."

"We can handle it," Charles insisted.

"Yeah, there are a lot more of us than there are of them," Matt added.

Kevin grabbed Jeff's arm. "How could you live with yourself, if something happened to Tracey and you didn't at least try?"

"How could I live with myself if something happened to one of you?" Jeff countered.

"Nothing's going to happen!"

"From your lips to God's ears. Come on, let's gather hands." They held on to each other a little tighter than usual, and Jeff prayed, pleading with God to protect Tracey and Willa, and to see them all through this ordeal safely.

He thought of Dawn, brutalized, her body dumped in some back alley by her pimp or a john, the cops couldn't say for sure. Her face—the way she had looked in the morgue—still haunted his dreams and kept him up at night. If only he'd done more to get through to her, if only he'd tried a little harder.

Was he making that same mistake again?

Anger surged through him. He clamped his fists, took three deep breaths, and pushed it back down. "I radioed for help. The rangers will be here soon."

"It will be dark soon," Lisa said quietly.

"What if we took the boat downriver?" Matt suggested. "We can get to the bottom of the trail a lot quicker than they can on foot."

"We'd never make it by nightfall," Jeff replied. Though he had to admit, he was leaning toward the idea.

"Nor will they," Kevin challenged.

"Yeah, and it will be easier to see in the dusk where they've set up camp," Matt added.

"And while they're sleeping we could grab Tracey and run," Charles insisted, pushing his glasses back farther on his nose.

Jeff had to grin. They were acting like this was some kind of Hollywood blockbuster rescue mission. But it wasn't. "I can't risk you kids."

"All right," Kevin conceded. "We'll stay in the boat on shore, and you can rescue her. Once you get her back to the boat, we'll take off down river. They'll never catch us."

Matt grabbed Willa's pack and took two steps toward the boat. "Yeah, and we can meet up with the rangers at Peterson's Flat."

"In the dark?" Jeff asked.

"How many times have you been down this river?

It won't be a problem. We'll light a lantern and go slowly,'' Kevin insisted.

Jeff knew this wasn't such a good idea. Knew it in the pit of his stomach, but he also knew they couldn't sit there and do nothing. ''You promise to stay in the boat when we find them?''

''Yes!'' All five heads nodded in unison.

''No renegade shenanigans?''

''Absolutely!''

''No action-hero-style heroics?''

''Yes!'' Kevin yelled, and with pack in hand ran toward the boat.

''Whoa, yeah,'' someone cheered.

''I mean it,'' Jeff insisted.

''Us, too,'' Charles agreed. ''Absolutely.''

''You're the boss man. All the way,'' Matt responded.

''Girls? I haven't heard much from you. Are you sure you want to do this?''

Monica and Lisa agreed wholeheartedly.

''All right. Let's do it.''

Within five minutes they'd gathered their supplies and were off paddling like mad, heading downriver, their eyes combing the shore for any sign of a campfire, Tracey or Willa.

Chapter Six

Willa trailed a good distance behind the trio, not letting them out of her sight. They showed no sign of slowing, and she could see Tracey was tired. The man with Carlos pushed her harder each time she stumbled.

And with each thrust, Willa's anger rose.

Tracey was just a kid. He had no right treating her in such a way. If she had her gun, she'd just take him out. Clean and easy. So much for all her years of training, she thought, but sometimes you gotta do what you gotta do.

If her dad had done that, he'd be alive today. But no, he'd had to follow proper procedure, he'd had to give a warning, he'd had to depend on his fellow officer. *He'd had to depend on Ben.* A bitter taste rose in her throat; she pushed it back down, concentrating on the scene before her.

She had to find a way to take out the guy doing the shoving. She picked up a medium-size branch and swung it like a club. It might work, if it didn't break on impact with his huge head. But if he didn't drop immediately, she and Tracey would be in even deeper trouble.

She should wait until they set up camp. One of them would probably rest while the other kept watch. It would be easier to take out one than two. But what if they didn't set up camp? What if they just pushed on even after dark? She should have brought Jeff's flashlight. She and Tracey were going to have a hard time escaping in total darkness. If not impossible.

No, she would have to do it now, before dark. *God, be with us,* she thought and, for a second, wondered where the thought had come from. Jeff. He was already rubbing off on her. She crept closer, keeping her gaze fixed on Tracey so Carlos or the thug wouldn't feel her stare.

"I'm tired," Tracey whined. "I need to rest." She and the goon were falling farther and farther behind Carlos.

"Keep moving," he demanded and gave her another shove.

Tracey fell to one knee.

"Get up!"

This was her chance! With all her might, Willa swung the makeshift club. Sensing her presence, he turned. The club impacted with the side of his face, instead of the back of his head as she'd intended. The force of the blow splintered the branch into several pieces. The man cried out and grabbed his head. Blood seeped through his fingers. Willa kicked him hard, sending him sprawling to the ground. She grabbed Tracey's hand and yelled, "Run!"

The two tore down the path as fast as they could.

But Tracey was already tired and Willa found herself having to pull her.

''Come on, sweetie. Carlos will be right behind us, and believe me, we don't want him to catch us.''

Tracey nodded and quickened her step.

They rounded the next bend. Tracey stumbled, righted herself and kept on, but her breathing was labored.

''I'm coming after you, Blondie!''

Willa shuddered at the sound of Carlos's voice. It sounded close. Too close. As they ran, she searched the surrounding area for a place to hide. There was no way they'd make it all the way back to Jeff.

''Why are you here?'' Tracey gasped between heavy breaths. ''I thought you led them to me. That you came to take me back.''

Willa looked back at the girl in astonishment. ''What in the world made you think that?''

''Why else would you be here?''

Why else indeed? ''It's true I tracked you down, but I didn't come for you, I came for the evidence against Paulson I'd hidden on Jeff.''

''Huh?''

''Never mind. It doesn't matter now. What matters is getting you to safety, and I can't do that if I'm yapping at you.''

Up a little farther off the trail to their left, Willa spotted what could be the answer to their problem. A series of large boulders sat stacked one atop the other and, from what she could tell, the backside of the rocks overhung the river.

''Blondie! I'm coming. I've almost got you now.''

Willa and Tracey skirted the rocks, then slipped into a crevice on the far side. Granite towered at least fifteen feet on three sides around them. It was a good hiding place, but if Carlos tracked them there, they'd be trapped.

"I'm going to give you a boost," she whispered. "Can you get your foot in that crack right there?" Willa pointed to the groove in the rocks where one boulder joined another.

Tracey nodded. "I think so."

"Let's give it a try, okay?" She linked her fingers, and bent over. Tracey stepped into her palms. Willa lifted, hoping the girl wouldn't fall backward. With splayed fingertips, Tracey clutched the side of the rock and climbed to the top.

"Peek out before exposing yourself," Willa whispered. She watched Tracey glance around, then disappear over the top of the boulders. Willa inserted her toe into a crevice, then pushed herself up the side of the rock.

"I'm coming for you, Blondie," Carlos taunted.

Willa froze. From the sound of his voice, she'd guess he was on the trail right outside the boulders. *Keep going down the path,* she urged silently. *Just keep on going.* She forced herself to count to ten before inching her way up the rock. As she reached the top, she saw Tracey huddled against a boulder, tears streaking down her cheeks.

"What is it?" Willa whispered.

Tracey pointed. Three feet to Willa's left, a large rattlesnake lay sleeping in a waning patch of sunlight. Willa's heart thumped painfully in her chest. What would they do now? A sinewy movement inched along the snake's coiled up body. The bottom dropped out of Willa's stomach. Her limbs clenched involuntarily. They needed to move. But where? If they went back down and Carlos came back, they'd be trapped. But up here, the snake had them trapped.

"Come on," Willa mouthed, afraid of making a sound. She inched backward, across the opening they just climbed up and across the rock toward the river. There weren't any large rocks blocking them on this side so if Carlos looked up from the trail he'd certainly spot them. But what choice did they have? She crept toward the far end of the rocks, hoping there would be a way to climb down the backside. Perhaps they could hide behind the rocks and hopefully, when the snake went down, it would go down the other way.

"Willa," Tracey called, her terrified voice barely above a whisper. The shimmy of a rattle sent fear flooding through Willa. Tracey was frozen, halfway across the rock a good four feet from the snake. Willa didn't know anything about snakes, but according to what she'd seen on the Nature Channel, the slithering little beasts could practically fly.

"Be careful, Tracey. Move toward me as slowly as you can."

"Well, well. What have we here?"

Willa cringed at the sound of Carlos's voice. She turned and looked down. Carlos was standing at the head of the trail, a huge grin splitting his ugly face.

"Shh," Matt cried, gesturing down with his hands. "I heard something."

"What?" Kevin asked.

"I don't know."

"I heard something, too," Charles agreed.

"A man's voice," Monica said. "It sounded like he said 'Blondie.'"

Jeff stopped rowing and held a finger to his lips. He looked around, his gaze searching the edge of the river. There wasn't a bank, just a massive rock cliff. He couldn't pull ashore here.

"I think we should get to the side. We're too easy to spot in the middle of the river," Kevin suggested.

Jeff agreed.

What had he been thinking, bringing the kids out here? He *hadn't* been thinking; that was the problem. All he could focus on was Tracey and Willa in the hands of those monsters, and the fact that he wasn't doing a thing about it. Silently, they guided the boat as close to the rocky ledge as they could. Long shadows from the cliff's edge fell over them.

"Maybe we should keep going," Kevin said. "We don't know how far sound travels out here. They could be another mile down the path."

"Let's just stay quiet a moment longer and perhaps we'll hear them again," Jeff said.

"Jeff, I'm scared," Lisa said, her eyes swimming with tears.

"I know, sweetheart." He put an arm around her back. "Me, too. But I'm not going to let anything happen to you. Any of you. Trust me?"

She nodded, sniffling.

He prayed it was a promise he could keep.

"What do you want from us, Carlos?"

''That's Willa's voice,'' Matt whispered.

Jeff's heart soared. It was! And she sounded close. He scanned the side of the cliff. They could be right above them. He had to find a way to get to shore, to help. He held a finger to his lips and pointed up the river to the only place he felt he'd be able to climb onto the rocks.

Kevin nodded, and without a sound rowed them back upstream.

If only Willa had a stick, that hissing snake would make a fine weapon dropped down on Carlos's head. Tracey continued inching backward, her gaze locked on the snake. Willa looked down. Carlos was on his way up to them, and they were stuck on the edge of the rocks with nowhere to go.

She'd hoped there would be another rock for them to leap down to, but no such luck. It was a sheer drop to the river below. She wondered if the rocks continued below the surface of the water, just in case they had to jump. But first, they had to escape the snake.

Carlos, no longer in sight, was probably climbing up the crevice wall.

''Willa—'' Tracey moaned.

The snake's coil tightened, his head standing at full attention. He opened his mouth, hissing as a forked tongue darted furiously across two venomous fangs.

''It's okay,'' Willa whispered. ''Just stay where you are. When Carlos reaches the opening, he'll divert the snake's attention. As soon as that happens, jump back behind me.''

''Will it bite him?''

"We can only hope."

"And pray."

"And pray," Willa agreed. This, she would pray for. "Dear God," she whispered out loud. "Please have that mighty serpent rear up its ugly head and bite Carlos right on the butt."

Tracey giggled in spite of herself, but neither of them took their eyes off the snake, or the opening in the rocks.

"Don't worry, Tracey. We're going to get out of this."

"How?"

"Can you swim?"

"Like a fish."

"Good."

Tracey's eyes widened as she looked back at her. "You want me to jump?"

"It's a possibility."

"But I can't! No way."

Carlos's head crested the rocks. He saw them and smiled—his grin evil. "Hey, Blondie. Looks like you're mine again."

"Don't count on it."

"Yep," he said and pushed himself higher, leaning over the rocks at his waist to get a better grip and pull himself up. Perhaps if she kicked him, he'd go flying backward. Yeah, and take her with him. "You and the pipsqueak are on my turf now, to do with whatever I want."

As Willa hoped, the snake turned toward Carlos.

"What the—"

Willa grabbed Tracey's arm and pulled. They both

hurried toward the edge of the rocks and stared down into the swirling river.

"I can't, Willa. I just can't."

"I know."

"Come on, God. If you're out there, now's your chance to prove it."

The snake lunged.

The loud smack of a gunshot echoed through the air. Willa heard a scream from below them, looked down, but didn't see anything. It sounded like one of the girls. Was it possible? The snake lay dead on the rocks, its head blown clean off.

Carlos laughed. "Nice try, Blondie. You're just full of surprises. I like women like you. Keeps the blood pumping."

"Jump!" Willa shouted.

Carlos leaped toward them onto their rock.

"No!"

Willa pushed her off the cliff. Tracey fell, shrieking all the way down to the water. Before Willa could follow, Carlos had his thick, meaty arm wrapped around her neck. The muzzle of the gun pushed against her temple.

"Stay still while Carlos has a little target practice with the ducky in the water."

"Let her go, Carlos. She's just a little kid."

When Tracey didn't surface, Willa feared she'd hit the rocks. She shouldn't have pushed her. They should have taken their chances up here.

"She doesn't look so little to me."

Tracey's head bobbed to the surface. Willa let out a deep breath.

"Where's the pen?" Carlos asked, his breath on her neck hot and foul.

"The what?" Willa answered with as much confusion as she could muster.

"You know what. Now give it to me, or I'll do to the kid what I did to the snake."

His body, pinned to hers, went rigid, and she knew what he was planning, knew it in an instant. As soon as he had the pen, he'd kill them both.

His hands moved roughly over her. If only she'd left the Pen Cam in her pack, but after showing it to Jeff, she'd slipped it in her back pocket.

"Ah, found it." He held up the Pen Cam and turned it on. "Let's make sure we get this all on camera for the boss to see."

He pointed the camera at Tracey in the water. "Here's the kid, boss." He grabbed Willa by the hair and yanked her head back, "and here's Blondie. Only she's not so blond without her wig. Say hi to the boss."

Willa didn't respond.

Carlos yanked her head back harder. "I said say hi, 'cause it's the last thing you're ever going to say."

She jumped at the cock of the gun's hammer, the cold steel burning a hole in her temple as he pushed the gun against her skin.

"Tracey, hide!" she screamed.

Carlos cracked the gun against her skull. Pain exploded in her head before darkness surrounded her.

Following their voices, Jeff made his way up the rock wall and reached the top just as Carlos brought the gun down on Willa's head. Anger exploded inside him as Willa wavered. He watched her grab hold of Carlos's shoulder. Blood trickled down the side of her face. The sight sent Jeff's mind spinning with rage. Carlos raised the gun again. Jeff cleared the opening and jumped onto the rock.

A huge snake lay dead in his path. Grabbing the snake, he hurled it at Carlos and lunged. Carlos dropped Willa long enough to ward off the snake's carcass. Before Willa could slump to the rocks, Jeff had her by the waist and jumped off the cliff.

Together they hit the cold water and sunk deep below the surface. He hung tight to Willa's hand and guided her toward the deepening shadows against the cliff's wall. They broke free to the surface and took a deep breath. Thankfully, Willa's eyes were wide-open and alert.

"Jeff?"

Relief mushroomed inside him. She was okay! "Shh," he said and looked up, expecting to see Carlos standing above them, a pistol in hand. But nothing could be seen above the rock's outcrop. A shot rang out and hit the water next to Jeff's head.

"Come on," he called, and went under again, towing Willa in the direction of the boat. Dull thuds sounded under the surface as more bullets broke through the water. He pulled them deeper. Willa tugged on his hand. Reluctantly, he let her lead them up for air.

They had to be close to the boat now. As they broke the surface, he saw the boat full of his kids, hiding in the shadows. Tracey sat in the back, a steady flow of tears running down her face. The fear expressed on all their faces clenched his stomach. Another shot rang out, but it wasn't anywhere near them.

''He'll have to come down for a better position. We don't have much time,'' Willa whispered. Quickly, they climbed into the boat.

''Push off, Kevin,'' Jeff ordered, and the boy pushed his oar against the shore with a mighty shove. The boat headed for the center of the river, and they all paddled as fast and furious as they could.

''I can't believe you guys are here.'' Tears filled Willa's eyes. ''Where did you come from?''

''We weren't about to let you rescue Tracey alone,'' Kevin huffed.

''Yeah, no way, man. We're a team,'' Charles said with certainty.

Jeff had never been more proud of anyone than he was of these kids right then.

Willa smiled. ''Well, thank you. We wouldn't have made it without you.''

''Just consider us your backup,'' Matt announced.

''Backup like you, I can always use.''

Another shot rang out, coming frighteningly close.

''Everyone get down,'' Jeff ordered, but no one listened. Instead they rowed harder and faster.

''This ain't over yet, Blondie!'' Carlos called from the shore. ''You can't escape me!''

''She already has, you bozo!'' Kevin yelled back.

Carlos shot at them again, but the bullet was a good six feet short. They were too far away now. They were safe. Or at least Jeff hoped they were as he watched the sky grow darker and darker. They couldn't afford to stop and set up camp. Carlos would easily find them if they did. They'd have to spend the night drifting downriver. Hopefully by morning they'd hit Peterson's Flat and find reinforcements waiting for them.

"I think we've made it," Jeff said. *Thank you, Lord.*

"Thanks to you," Willa added, and gave his arm a squeeze.

"Ah, it was nothing, ma'am."

"It was everything. It was more than I'll ever be able to repay."

He smiled, and found himself hoping she'd try. "I'm just thankful we're all safe."

"Me, too. Except…"

"What?"

"I lost the evidence."

"You and Tracey made it out alive. That's all that matters."

Willa nodded. "Carlos didn't get us this time, but he was right about one thing."

"What's that?"

"This definitely isn't over."

Chapter Seven

Willa had been rowing as fast and as hard as she could for at least thirty minutes, and that was a good twenty minutes longer than she thought she could. She swatted a mosquito off her cheek, and gnawed her bottom lip. Nothing had gone as she'd planned. All she had to do was pick up a small piece of evidence, nothing too big or too difficult. And she'd blown it.

And in the process, she'd put the lives of Jeff and these poor kids on the line. She looked into their scared and tired faces. This was supposed to have been a great trip for them, fun and exciting, and she ruined it. Carlos had tracked her down.

What would Ben have to say to her now? She shook her head, fighting back the despair that threatened to overwhelm her. He'd say she let him down. She wasn't the cop she could be. She wasn't anything like her dad.

"I don't feel so good," Monica moaned.

A shot echoed through the trees. Willa looked up.

Charles jumped. ''Where'd that come from?''

''Carlos. He's letting us know he's still there,'' Willa answered.

Lisa started to cry again.

''It's all right. We're not in range. He can't hurt you. He can't hurt any of you,'' Willa reassured them, though she didn't completely believe it. Look at all the damage he'd already caused.

Monica threw up over the side of the boat. Matt and Kevin groaned in protest.

''Are you all right?'' Willa asked and rubbed the girl's back. Monica nodded without lifting her head off the side of the boat. Willa met Jeff's eyes over the kids' heads. This situation was going from bad to worse. And from the expression on Jeff's face, he didn't have any suggestions.

They floated downstream in silence, listening as the nocturnal nightlife moved into full swing.

''Do we have anything to eat?'' Matt asked.

''I left a lot back at the campsite, but I do have granola bars,'' Jeff offered.

Matt shrugged. ''Sounds good to me.''

Jeff passed them around, and lit the lantern as the last vestiges of light disappeared. Willa strained her eyes to see past the lantern's glow as the night grew darker. ''Are you sure rafting in the dark is safe?'' she asked.

''Our friend hasn't left us too many choices. We need to put as much distance between ourselves and him as possible.''

Another shot sounded in the distance. ''I see you,

Blondie!'' His mocking laughter sent chills skittering down her spine.

Tracey gasped. ''How can he keep up with us?''

''I'm sure he can spot this lantern from a mile away. Sounds carry out here. He probably isn't that close,'' Jeff responded.

Willa wasn't so sure. If Carlos was anything, he was relentless and insanely motivated. This had become a cat-and-mouse game for him and he was having the time of his disgusting life. ''Do we need the lantern on?'' Willa asked as casually as she could.

''Absolutely. I have to be able to see if there is anything in our path—rocks, driftwood, whatever.''

''We're like sitting ducks out here,'' Kevin stated.

''Not if we can get far enough ahead of him,'' Jeff responded.

Monica threw up again and started to cry.

''What if we can't outrun him?'' Tracey asked, echoing the words racing through Willa's mind.

Willa scooped up a handful of water and washed Monica's face. She looked up in alarm. ''Jeff, she's burning up.''

Jeff moved to the front of the boat, and felt Monica's head. ''What's wrong, sweetie?''

''I don't feel good,'' she answered weakly. ''The boat's rocking is making me sick.''

''We have to get her off this boat,'' Willa said, though she knew they couldn't. As soon as they went ashore, Carlos would find them.

''Where would we go?'' Tracey asked. ''We can't take the chance he'll find us again. We just can't.''

A huge grin crossed Kevin's face. ''I know where.''

Everyone in the boat stared at him.

"Care to enlighten us?" Jeff asked.

Kevin fluttered his fingers. "The bat cave."

Willa eyes widened in alarm. "The what?"

"Last year, we stopped for lunch along the shore and discovered a cave filled with bats. Remember? There were thousands of them. It was really cool."

To Willa's absolute horror, she could see Jeff was contemplating the idea.

"Yeah," Matt added. "If we hid in there, we could light a fire and that guy would never see it."

Jeff stroked his jaw. "It could work," he agreed.

"I don't think so." The thought of sleeping in a cave with thousands of bats hanging over her head, ignited a fierce sense of revulsion in Willa's stomach unlike anything she'd ever felt before. "I think I'm going to be sick, too. In fact, I'm sure of it."

"That settles it," Jeff decided. "The cave is about an hour downriver from here. I don't think Monica can take much more than that in this boat, and hopefully our psycho won't be able to keep up with us for that long."

"But bats?" she protested.

"Ah, come on, Willa," Matt cajoled. "You're not afraid, are you?"

Charles pushed his glasses up higher on his nose. "They're fascinating, really."

"Of course I'm not afraid," Willa responded. "I just don't like rodents. Especially flying rodents," she muttered under her breath.

"They're cool," Kevin added, and plastered his

face with one of those smug expressions only a teenager could master.

"I'm sure they'll all be out flying around soon, hunting, eating, doing their bat thing," Tracey added.

Something whooshed by above them. Willa snapped up her head and stared into the darkness, goose bumps breaking out all over her skin.

"Yeah. The more I think about it, the more I like the idea," Kevin stated.

"Do you think you'd remember how to get there, if we managed to find the place we stopped along the river?" Matt asked Jeff.

Hope surged through Willa. It was dark, how could he possibly remember the exact spot?

Tracey leaned forward. "It was right next to that huge tree whose branches hung down into the water, remember? I called it Mother Willow."

The girl was beginning to perk up, and from the lantern's light, Willa could see the gleam of adventure replacing desperation in her eyes. All right, she supposed she could handle one night of bats. And it would be nice to have a fire. She rubbed her arms and realized it was getting cold.

"All right," Willa agreed reluctantly. "A fire would be nice."

"Then we'll put our fate in your hands, big man," Jeff stated and patted Kevin on the back.

"How long would it take us to get to Peterson's Flat if we just stayed in the boat and kept drifting?" Lisa asked.

"Six or seven hours."

Willa shivered and rubbed her arms, then picked up her oar.

Monica leaned her head over the side and threw up once more. Willa put more muscle into her rowing, and strained her eyes in the dimness for the huge tree with the long flowing branches that reached deep into the water.

Willa wasn't sure what she'd expected, but this wasn't it. "It's so small," she said, and peered doubtfully into the four-foot opening.

"Exactly," Matt announced. "A perfect hiding place."

"Yeah, you'd never find it if you didn't already know it was here," Kevin added.

Willa looked around her and realized she'd rather stay outside than enter the claustrophobic hole. "How many bats did you say were in there?"

"Thousands, millions," Kevin answered.

The laughter in his voice was beginning to grate on her nerves. "And why do we want to go in there again?"

"Because it's cold and we need to build a fire where it won't be seen and Monica needs to rest. Stop stalling and help me out," Jeff stated.

Was that annoyance she detected?

"Yeah, stop being such a scaredy-cat and come on, Willa," Kevin added.

She wondered if anyone would notice if she tripped him in the dark. She was not a scaredy-cat. She just didn't like cohabiting with sharp-clawed flying rodents in extremely dark small spaces.

She bent over and followed the kids through the opening and continued deep into the cave. The damp, earthy smell was almost overwhelming. She stumbled and immediately reached out her arms, scraping her knuckles on each wall flanking her.

Her boots sloshed in a muck-filled hole, and for the first time since this dreaded weekend began, she was thankful for her stiff leather boots. A spasm tore at her shoulders, and she hoped the ceiling would rise soon. After about twenty feet, Jeff switched on the flashlight; its dim glow eased the panic surging within her chest.

Soon they reached a nice-size chamber where she could stand upright. With reluctance, Willa glanced up and was able to see a few inverted bats hanging above them. They didn't appear so threatening. In fact they didn't look big enough to cause any trouble at all. Suddenly, she felt a little foolish. Perhaps she *was* a little bit of a scaredy-cat.

Jeff shone the flashlight along the wall to their left where a small crevice jutted into the wall. "We'll have to sleep in there," he stated, shining his light along the small space in the wall.

Within minutes, Jeff had a small fire crackling. Immediately, the tension dropped out of her shoulders and a smile hovered on her lips. She took a step toward the warm flames. Suddenly, a loud roar of flapping wings and high-pitched squeaks pierced her ears. She squatted low as the remaining bats vacated the cave in a furious flurry.

"I guess they didn't like the light," Lisa stated.

"Or the smoke," Jeff added.

Willa stilled her hammering heart and watched as

wisps of smoke rose to the top of the cave then drifted down the shallow opening. She hoped it wasn't noticeable outside the cave. What if Carlos was near? Would he be able to smell it? If he discovered their hiding place, this time they really would be trapped. And she was ninety-nine-point-nine percent sure their bodies would never be found.

Jeff and the kids climbed into the crevice, joined hands and bowed their heads. "Dear Lord," he began.

"Wait," Tracey interrupted and held out her hand for Willa. She glanced once more toward the opening of the cave, then squeezed her way into the small enclosure next to Tracey. She took the girl's hand. The gracious approval in Jeff's expression moved something deep within her and, for just a second, joy warmed her.

"Dear Lord, thank you for bringing all of us safely through this day and providing us with this shelter. Please, watch over us, your children, through the rest of our journey. We remain faithfully yours. In Jesus' name, Amen."

"Amen," the kids responded.

Monica laid her head on Willa's leg, her small face pale and miserable. Willa stroked her hair back from her forehead, and was thankful when the girl's breathing evened. She watched the glow from the ebbing flames play across their young, innocent faces. "You have all been so brave. I'm very impressed by all of you."

"Do you think that man will find us in here?" Lisa asked, the fear evident in her voice.

"I find it very unlikely that Carlos or anyone would

be able to find us in here, and by morning the police will be out in full force searching for us. Carlos must realize that. I'm sure he's hightailed it out of here by now."

"So you can all sleep peacefully tonight," Jeff added.

"Do you really think so?" Tracey asked, her voice sounding hopeful.

Willa smiled reassuringly. "I know so."

"And so do I," Jeff said. "We've had an intense day, and you were all wonderful. I'm very proud of you, but for now the danger's over. We all need to get a good night's sleep. I'm sorry I didn't have time to grab more sleeping bags."

"It's cool," Kevin answered and gave his to Tracey. He then shared with Matt. The others had their own and Jeff slipped the last one over Monica and Willa. Warmth seeped into her chilled bones and for the first time since entering the cave, Willa realized just how cold she'd been. She stared into the dying flames and hoped what she'd said was true. Hoped Carlos was long gone and they'd have an uneventful and peaceful night.

She caught Jeff's warm gaze. He'd saved her. He could have grabbed Tracey and rowed away, but he didn't. He came through for her. They all did. He was incredible, and unlike anyone she'd ever met before. In fact, if she ever were to give a man a chance to get close to her, it would be someone like him. She sighed. Would he want the chance, if she gave it to him? She watched the fire's light dance across his face. He was everything any woman could ever want in a man: kind, caring, considerate, and drop-dead gorgeous.

Absolutely perfect.

Why would someone like that want to be with someone like her? Perfect was one feat she just couldn't seem to master.

"I think they've all dropped off to sleep," he whispered.

She nodded and offered him a small smile. "Thanks for the rescue."

"Anytime," he replied, and gave her that crooked grin that had her feeling all warm and fuzzy inside. "Carlos is gone. He won't find us here."

"Oh, good," Tracey murmured, and turned over in her bag.

Willa hoped he was right. Still, she and Jeff should take turns keeping watch, and as soon as she was sure the kids were asleep she would recommend just that. In the meantime, she'd rest her eyes for just a second. They stung with grit and exhaustion and it felt so good to close them. That was the last conscious thought she had.

Until a horrible sound woke her.

At first she wasn't sure what it could be. Her body ached and she was so tired, wakefulness didn't come easily. Something brushed against her cheek. Her eyes popped open, but she couldn't see anything but inky blackness. Air whooshed across her face. Something rustled overhead. Her heart pounded ferociously, knowing even before her brain had awakened enough to comprehend what was happening.

"Oh, no," she moaned.

"It's the bats, they've come back!" Kevin said.

"Shh, don't say anything," Jeff warned.

"This is so cool," Matt announced.

A bat caught the top of Willa's hair. She screamed, flailing her arms in the darkness.

"Shh," Jeff responded. "It's okay." He flipped on the flashlight. Masses of bats flew into the chamber, their eyes glowing red and yellow in the light's reflection. Terror gripped a tight hold on Willa's heart. She helped Monica to her feet and holding on to her waist, hurried her toward the cave's entrance.

Or at least she hoped they were heading out the right way, but she had to admit she wasn't exactly sure. More whooshing, more bats. She ducked down and swallowed another scream.

"What's happening?" Monica cried.

"The bats are coming back," she yelled above the thundering of wings.

They turned round a bend, then saw a faint light at the end of the tunnel. With the light, Willa could see the black cloud, surging through the cave's opening. She ducked down even lower, cringing each time a bat brushed up against her. Everyone ran as fast as they could out of the cave.

Outside, they stood upright and inhaled deep breaths of fresh air. The sun hadn't risen yet, though the sky grew lighter with each passing second. She should have brought the sleeping bag with them, she thought as Monica shivered against her.

"That was so awesome," Kevin exclaimed as he came running out of the cave, followed close behind by Matt and Charles.

Willa smiled at their enthusiasm, though where it came from she couldn't even pretend to imagine.

"Totally," Charles agreed.

"Yeah, awesome," Matt added. "I can't wait to tell everyone about this!"

Next came Tracey and Lisa, then finally Jeff wrapped in a sleeping bag. Monica and Willa ran toward him. He opened his arms and they both snuggled close. As the warmth flooded her bones, Willa wiggled closer, at once conscious of hard muscles beneath soft flannel and the heat of his skin through the fabric.

Her heart kicked up a beat and her breathing grew shallow. The others were talking excitedly, but their words weren't registering. Everything slipped away except a heightened awareness of Jeff's warmth, his all-male scent and the rough hairs growing on his face.

Willa dropped her head onto his shoulder. She didn't want to move, not ever.

"Come on," he whispered in her hair. "Let's get back to the boat."

No, she wanted to protest. For just that minute, she wanted to relish his warmth, accept his comfort and believe for just a second that in his arms the world was safe and whole and happy.

He started to walk and shattered the illusion.

By the soft gray light of dawn, the trail to the river wasn't nearly as long as it had seemed the night before. They found the boat easily. All was as they'd left it with no sign that Carlos had found them. They climbed into the boat and rowed slowly downriver, enjoying the crisp morning air, the chirping of the birds and the sight of the sun rising into the sky.

Willa couldn't stop reliving the feel of her body snuggled next to Jeff's. The urge to wrap her arms around his waist and nestle her face into the warm crook of his neck was almost more than she could bear. She had grown very fond of him, but what would happen once they returned home? Would she ever be wrapped in his arms again?

She remembered his statement that he didn't get down to her part of town often and felt a deep ache. No, she supposed this was the last time she'd see him.

It wasn't long before they heard the rumble of a helicopter. Willa watched the kids wave and cheer as it flew overhead. The pilot waved back, then circled the area as he looked for a flat spot to land. They rowed toward shore as a ranger in rescue gear jumped out of the back of the helicopter and ran toward them. "Reverend MacPhearson?" he yelled as they departed the boat. "You all all right?"

"We're all fine," Jeff yelled back.

The ranger gestured for them to follow him into the helicopter. They ran as the air from the blades whipped their hair. Willa stared out the window as they soared above the tips of the trees and watched the wilderness slip by beneath them. Why wasn't she happy? Relieved? They were safe. Instead she felt sad and miserable. It was just an emotional night, that's all, she thought as they followed the line of the river. It had nothing to do with missing Jeff and these kids.

"Some of the kids' folks are waiting by the van," the ranger announced. "The others have congregated at your church and will wait for you there." No one said a word at his news. She hoped she wouldn't have to explain to frantic parents why a thug like Carlos had terrorized their kids all night. Within ten minutes she spotted her Jeep and they were landing on a main road that had been barricaded to stop the flow of traffic.

"We're back!" Kevin whooped.

"Yes! Civilization," Charles agreed.

"Warm beds," Monica announced.

Matt smiled and rubbed his stomach. "Bacon, eggs and T.V."

A hot shower, Willa thought with a small smile. She could just imagine how lovely she must look and smell, sleeping in a cave full of bat droppings.

She watched Monica, Lisa and Charles run to their parents and embrace. Jeff spoke softly to them, assuring them that their children were fine. She wondered how this trip would affect him and if this would be the last wilderness excursion the church would allow.

A policeman quietly approached her. "Officer Barrett?"

"Yes."

"Do you want to tell me what happened up there?"

She briefly told him what had happened after Matt saw Carlos and his partner take Tracey. "Carlos is probably long gone by now."

"And what about his partner?"

"I didn't see him again after I hit him."

"Do you think he's dead?"

"No."

"All right, we'll look for him. You got a description?"

Willa called Matt over. "Can you draw a picture of the man you saw take Tracey?"

Eagerly, Matt nodded and opened his pad. He furrowed his brow in concentration as his pencil flew across the page. As he worked, Willa described Carlos's partner to the officer. After a few minutes, Matt held up his pad. A graphite image of Carlos stared back at her. Even though she was prepared for it, seeing his anger emblazoned on paper turned her stomach.

"This is good," the officer said. "Can I have it?"

"Thanks," Matt replied, beaming. He ripped off the page and handed it to the officer.

Willa tousled his hair. "You were wonderful out there."

"So were you." The admiration shining in his eyes touched her. Maybe kids weren't so bad after all. *Especially these kids.* She looked over at Jeff and felt a heaviness in her chest. Neither were youth ministers.

"I'll get this on the wire right away."

"As far as I know, he still resides on Sunset in L.A. Did anyone contact Captain Armstrong there? They can keep watch for him."

"Yep, filled him in soon as we heard they found you. He said to tell you to get your derriere back asap and not to forget the evidence."

"Well, then if we're done, er, I'll do just that."

"What evidence was he referring to?"

"It doesn't matter. I lost it."

"Oh." He nodded, and this time added a chuckle. "Then, I guess I wouldn't want to be in your shoes just now."

''Nope, I guess you wouldn't.'' Willa hopped into her Jeep and started the engine. Jeff was talking to a group of worried parents. She should wait for him and say goodbye, should thank him one more time. But for some reason she couldn't fathom, she felt on the verge of crying. And she was afraid that one kind, wonderful word from him, and she'd be done for. She slid the gearshift into reverse and started to back out of the parking lot, but stopped as Jeff waved and ran over.

She took a deep breath and rolled down the window.

''Would you mind meeting us at the church later? I'd like you to be there when we explain what happened out here.''

Willa's stomach filled with dread. ''Sure. What exactly should we say?''

''As little about Tracey as possible.''

She glanced toward the girl and saw her back away from the group and realized how isolated she must be feeling, and how embarrassed. ''Would she like to ride back with me?''

Jeff looked surprised. ''I don't know. But I'll ask.'' He trotted over and posed the question to Tracey. Willa saw her look from Jeff to Willa's Jeep then back to Jeff, her head nodding, and a grateful look crossing her face.

Jeff gave her the thumbs-up sign. She smiled and nodded.

Tracey ran to the Jeep and climbed in. ''Thanks, Willa.''

''Sure thing. I thought you could use a break from the others.''

''You got that right.''

Jeff approached her window and handed her a card with the directions to the church scribbled on the back. "I'll see you in about five hours."

"If you don't mind, we're going to stop at my place for a shower before going to the church. I can't stand the smell of myself a moment longer than I have to."

He grinned. "All right. We'll take an extra long time when we stop for breakfast." He looked at his watch. "It's seven thirty a.m. now. How about we meet at the church about one-thirty?"

"You got it."

He placed his hands on her door and leaned in. "Thanks, Willa."

He was so close. She wished she could touch him. "For what?"

"For being there."

"That was a fluke. And if I hadn't been there, Carlos wouldn't have tracked us down."

"We don't know that." He looked past her at Tracey.

"Yes, I do," Willa responded. "I let Carlos find me, I let him know I had the Pen Cam and I led him right to you."

Jeff nodded stoically, then placed his hands on her shoulder. "Don't be so hard on yourself. You're an awesome cop, and one terrific lady." His eyes held hers and, for a moment, she thought she'd cry.

"Thank you," she whispered, and squeezed his hand.

"Be safe, both of you. You're precious cargo."

"Always," she said, then as he stepped away, she backed up and drove away. No one had ever spoken to her like that before. *He doesn't care about you in* that way, she reminded herself. He's from a different world, a different life. She didn't have a chance with someone like him.

She took a deep breath and turned to Tracey. "Any idea what you're going to tell your mom?"

"Everything, I guess. What choice do I have?"

"Not much."

"Thanks for agreeing to be there with me. You can tell her that nothing happened. That I didn't do anything."

"No, you didn't. Of course I'll tell her."

Tracey chewed on her lip.

Willa frowned. "What is it?"

"They didn't come after us because of you, Willa. They came after me. They came to get this back." Tracey pulled a wad of bills out of her pocket. "It's the five hundred dollars Mr. Paulson gave me. I never gave it back to him."

"Oh." Willa stared at the crisp one-hundred-dollar bills. "Believe me, sweetie, he didn't just come for that. There's a Baggie in the glove box. Can you put the money in it? We can use it as evidence against him."

"Really?"

"Yep. But that means you'll have to testify because Carlos got the pen. Do you think you can do that?"

"Testify? Like on T.V.? 'Do you swear to tell the truth, the whole truth, and nothing but the truth?' That kind of testify?"

"Yep. That's what I mean. Only it's not nearly as interesting as it is on T.V."

"Oh. Yeah, I guess I can do that."

"Good, because right now you're all we've got."

Chapter Eight

Willa felt Tracey stiffen as they pulled into the rectory parking lot at exactly 1:30 p.m. She heard Tracey's deep breath and took one of her own as she killed the ignition. "Everything will be just fine," she said with more confidence than she felt.

She took the girl's hand and gave it a reassuring squeeze. A small group of people were huddled in the rectory speaking quietly. A tall woman spotted them as they approached.

"Tracey, thank God!" she cried, and ran to embrace her.

Willa's heart lifted at the relief shining through Tracey's face. No admonishments or blame, just a big hug. Wasn't that what they all needed? Willa spotted Jeff smiling at her. He'd showered and shaved off the two-day growth. She'd grown rather fond of the stubble. Now he looked too clean-cut for someone like her.

She shook the thought out of her head. Of course he was clean-cut. He was a minister and this was his church, his world. And a beautiful world it was. Everywhere she looked golden wood polished to a warm shine greeted her. There would be no yelling here, no cursing, no one complaining about bitter coffee or anything else.

She wasn't sure she could stand it.

"Mom, this is Willa. She saved my life," Tracey said, interrupting her thoughts.

Evelyn Wilcox grabbed Willa in a crushing embrace. "I don't know what I would have done if I'd lost my daughter, too. There aren't words to express my gratitude. Thank you so much."

"It was a team effort. We all pitched in and made it work together."

"God blessed my Tracey when he sent you," she stated and kissed Willa's cheek.

Outwardly Willa smiled, but inside she cringed. God cursed Tracey when he'd sent her. And soon everyone would know it. She'd bungled this case, and now with the evidence in Carlos's hands, Tracey would have to testify against Jack in court. The thought sickened her. If Jack could find them in a vast national forest, how long would it take him to find Tracey's house, right here in Pasadena?

She had to inform Evelyn that Tracey needed to come to the station and give a statement. They would have to find somewhere safe to stay, somewhere no one knew about. It broke Willa's heart to tell her—to put the fear back into her eyes.

But she did what she had to do.

She pulled out a card and scribbled her home number on the back. ''Call me as soon as you're settled and let me know how to reach you.''

Mrs. Wilcox nodded gravely and left, hurrying Tracey out of the church.

''This is the lady I told you about,'' Jeff explained to two older gentlemen as they approached. ''Willa Barrett, please meet our head Pastor James Williamson and my father, Pastor Edward MacPhearson.''

Willa felt herself shrinking to microscopic size under the intense scrutiny of Jeff's father. ''It's a pleasure to meet you,'' she said finally.

Pastor Williamson took her hand within his own and graciously thanked her for her help on the mountain. His warmth was sincere and for that Willa was thankful. Jeff's father, on the other hand, wasn't so warm or sincere. His hawklike gaze judged her relentlessly and, by the set of his jaw, she sensed she wasn't measuring up.

''Jeff's been telling us how you saved the day, Miss Barrett,'' Mr. MacPhearson stated.

''He exaggerated, I'm sure.'' She smiled warmly, hoping to melt his icy exterior. ''Truth is, Jeff and the kids saved us by coming after Tracey and me.''

''A chance a more practical, and perhaps less reckless, pastor wouldn't have taken, but in your case it turned out to be most prudent.''

Willa's eye's widened at the insult. Quickly, she looked to Jeff who stood rigid. ''The fact remains that Tracey and I wouldn't have made it back without him.''

''I think you're being modest, my dear. You are a trained professional, aren't you?''

''Yes, but—''

''And I understand you pose as a—'' he cleared his throat over the distasteful word ''—prostitute?''

Jeff stepped forward, but Willa stopped him with a hand to his arm. ''That's right, Mr. MacPhearson. I do whatever I can to clean the dirt off the streets and sometimes, to do a good job, I've got to roll up my sleeves and get a little dirty.''

His eyes narrowed and he turned to Jeff, dismissing her. ''I must be leaving. You're very fortunate everything turned out...beneficial.'' He placed his right hand on Jeff's shoulder and looked him square in the eye. ''This time.''

''Goodbye, Dad,'' Jeff said stiffly and they all watched in silence as he walked out the door.

''Let's join the others for a bite to eat,'' Pastor Williamson said and hooked his arm through Willa's and led her into an oversize kitchen.

Willa eyed the trays of sandwiches, fruit, vegetables and cheese and crackers.

''We thought you might be hungry. We're having a barbecue next Sunday with the whole congregation. We'd love it if you could join us, so we can thank you properly for helping young Jeff with the children.''

''Oh, believe me, Jeff didn't need any help from me.''

''Some of the parents had concerns about the children going so far away and to such a remote place, but we've had so much success with the trips in the past, that we never dreamed there would be a problem like this. Now, I'm afraid we'll have to keep our outings a little more local, and a lot more supervised.'' He picked up a cracker and nibbled the corner.

Willa noticed Jeff's jaw harden and knew how much the pastor's words had upset him. Her heart ached for him. *If only I'd stayed away from you, none of this would have happened.* ''That's too bad,'' she responded. ''The trip was so good for the kids. They got along together well and really loosened up and talked. It was truly inspiring and wonderful to watch.''

''That's very sweet of you to say, dear,'' he said, patting her shoulder before stuffing a green olive into his mouth.

A spark of rebellion ignited in Willa's blood. What was wrong with these people? Didn't they know what a wonderful pastor Jeff was? What a wonderful man? She'd better leave, and soon before she said something she'd regret. A church was no place for her.

''Willa?'' Jeff touched her shoulder; his gaze was soft and gentle. Something warm fluttered in her chest, calming the irritation growing inside her.

''Would you like a tour?''

His voice caressed the rough edges of her nerves. ''Yes, I would.'' Actually, she couldn't care less about the church grounds, but she liked the joy she felt just looking in his eyes and she didn't want the feeling to stop. She wasn't ready to say goodbye. Not to him. Not yet.

They walked from room to room, through pristine offices and Sunday school classrooms. ''I apologize for my father. He usually isn't so rude. He…he means well.''

''Don't they all? I mean, it's amazing the horrible

things said and done in the name of love. Not that your dad has done horrible things or anything,'' she corrected quickly.

He laughed. ''It's okay, I know what you mean. I'm afraid you represent a side of town my dad wants me to stay away from.''

''Yeah, inner-city L.A. isn't as scrubbed or genteel as Pasadena.''

''Before I came here, I worked at a parish down off the strip, only a few miles from where we picked up Tracey.''

''You're kidding? You mean Sun Valley?''

''That's the one. You've heard of it?''

''Of course! They've been doing wonderful things for the runaways.''

''That's the program I helped start.'' His tone was wistful.

''What happened? Why'd you leave?''

''I lost a young girl. I wasn't able to reach her. She ran away again and returned to the strip, worked a few tricks, and...unfortunately was murdered.''

''I'm sorry.''

''They never found her killer. I'm afraid I've let her death color a lot of the decisions I've made.''

''Knowing you did everything you possibly could?''

''Did I? I like to think so, but I'll always wonder.''

Willa stopped walking and placed her hand on his arm. ''I realize I've only known you for a couple of days, but those were pretty intense days. I know you gave that girl everything you had, because that's the kind of man you are. You don't hold back. It's all or

We'd like to send you two free books to introduce you to Love Inspired®. Your two books have a combined cover price of $9.50 in the U.S. and $11.50 in Canada, but they are yours free! We'll even send you a wonderful surprise gift. You can't lose!
HEARTWARMING INSPIRATIONAL ROMANCE
Love Inspired
SONG OF HER HEART
IRENE BRAND
LONG WAY HOME
GENA DALTON
THE HARBOR OF HIS ARMS
LYNN BULOCK
SWEET ACCORD
FELICIA MASON
LOVING HEARTS
GAIL GAYMER MARTIN
Each of your FREE books is filled with joy, faith and traditional values as men and women open their hearts to each other and join together on a spiritual journey
FREE BONUS GIFT!
We'll send you a wonderful surprise gift, absolutely FREE, just for giving Love Inspired® books a try! Don't miss out—
MAIL THE REPLY CARD TODAY!
Order online at:
www.LoveInspiredBooks.com

HURRY!

Return this card promptly to get ***2 FREE Books*** *and a* ***FREE Bonus Gift!***

YES! *Please send me the 2 FREE Love Inspired® books and FREE gift for which I qualify. I understand that I am under no obligation to purchase anything further, as explained on the back and on the opposite page.*

affix free books sticker here

▼ DETACH AND MAIL CARD TODAY! ▼

313 IDL DVG4 113 IDL DVG3

FIRST NAME LAST NAME

ADDRESS

APT.# CITY

STATE/PROV. ZIP/POSTAL CODE

Steeple Hill®

™ Offer limited to one per household and not valid to current subscribers of Love Inspired® books. All orders subject to approval. Books received may not be as shown. Credit or debit balances in a customer's account(s) may be offset by any other outstanding balance owed by or to the customer.

LI-FL-04

nothing with you. I can see that, and so can the kids. That's why they love and trust you.''

A smile lit his eyes, chasing away the shadows of regret. ''Thanks. I guess I needed to hear that after this weekend's disaster.''

''You're welcome. You deserve it.'' *And so much more.* He was such a good man, the best she'd ever met. And this weekend wouldn't have been a disaster if it hadn't have been for her.

They entered a fabulous rose garden blooming in a riot of color. She stopped to touch a lavender petal. ''So how did you get from there to a place like this?''

''Dad pulled some strings. I'm afraid his ambitions for me are a bit loftier than the ones I have for myself.''

''And you caved?''

''Not exactly how I'd put it, but the end result was the same.''

''Sorry. Not that this isn't a nice place to spend your days, beautiful in fact, pristine, manicured...perfect.''

''Too perfect?''

''Just for a very unperfect person like me.''

He laughed. ''You, Miss Willa Barrett, are absolutely perfect.''

Warmth flooded her cheeks. ''Thanks. Now if you could just convince my boss of that.''

''Worried?''

''I'm afraid he's not going to take the news that I lost the evidence very well.''

''But you saved Tracey.''

''He won't see it that way. All he'll see is that I almost got her killed. In two days' time, I managed to bring the wrath of Jack Paulson down on one youth minister and six children. The fact that we survived won't matter much.''

''It matters to me.''

''Yeah, I know,'' she said and grinned.

''If he doesn't appreciate your many talents, you could always get a job as a ranger or tour guide in Sequoia.''

''Yeah, right!'' She laughed, and it felt good to loosen up.

''Hey, you were a wilderness pro by the time we left that bat cave.''

''A night I'll never forget.''

''Me, either,'' he said, his tone at once serious. He stepped closer. Their eyes locked. Was he going to kiss her? Did she want him to? Oh, yes. Her lids lowered, her chin lifted.

''You were God's gift to Tracey, and to me.'' His words, as if coming down a long tunnel, whispered across her mind. Her gaze fell on soft, mussed hair brushing across his ears, then lowered to his thick neck broadening into line-backer shoulders. He was incredible. And he was speaking.

''I'm sorry, you were saying?''

''I've thanked God a hundred times that he brought you to us. You were there for Tracey, not only in the forest, but in Jack's building, too. Keep that thought in your mind when you face your captain.''

''You're kind. Thank you, I will.'' With disappointment, she realized he wasn't going to kiss her. What made her think he would? That they could have a chance anyhow? She could never fit into his world. Slowly, they made their way to the parking lot.

"Will you accompany me to the church barbecue this weekend?"

She looked past him, into the picture-perfect gardens of the rectory and tried to imagine it filled with parishioners each knowing her story, each knowing how she blew it out there on top of that mountain. "I don't know. Can I get back to you on that?"

"Sure."

"It's just, well, it depends what the captain has in store for me. I might be chained to a desk or something."

He smiled. "Okay."

"If I can't, maybe we can do coffee or dinner?"

"You got it."

She climbed into her Jeep, gave him a small wave and watched him walk away, certain she would never hear from him again.

News sure did travel fast, Willa thought as she walked through the station house. Officers were staring at her, the look on their faces a mixture of pity and I-told-you-so condemnation. She took a deep breath and sighed. A few days ago their looks wouldn't have bothered her, but today she felt more alone than ever.

She gave one of the older cops she'd known since she was a child a small smile. He didn't smile back, but instead patted her shoulder as she headed into Ben's office.

"Hi, Captain," she said, and dropped into the Chair of Disapproval.

He clasped his hands on his desk and looked at her, his direct gaze scrutinizing every molecule of her being. "All you had to do was take a little hike up to where they'd be camping, pick up the evidence, and deliver it back here to me. Wasn't that how it was supposed to go down?"

"Things happen, sir."

"Especially when *you're* involved. Give me the Pen Cam, Willa. This evidence better be worth the public scrutiny this department is going to receive over this latest escapade of yours."

She took a deep breath to gather her confidence, then looked him directly in the eye. "I don't have it, sir."

He stared at her, his gaze hardening, his brows coming together to form a single line. "You want to run that by me again?"

"Carlos took it from me."

He was silent, fuming like an animated Saturday morning cartoon character. She could practically see the steam flowing from his nose and ears.

"I apologize, Captain. But the girl is willing to testify, and we do have an eye witness who can identify Carlos as the kidnapper."

"They're kids."

"I know." She searched for something more to add that would remove the disappointment from his face, though she wasn't sure why it bothered her so much. "But they're great kids," she offered weakly.

"I've scheduled you to start meeting with Louis

next Monday, and you *will* make those appointments.''

Defiance narrowed her eyes. But the captain wasn't playing. He'd given up on her. ''But—''

''And frankly, at this point I don't even care if you go. You have a choice, you can put what happened to your father behind you and move on with your life, forming healthy relationships with people, or you can stew in revenge plots forever. It doesn't matter to me. I'm not going to spend another sleepless night worrying about you. Is that clear?''

''Yes. I'm sorry,'' she said softly. He'd been worried about her? The thought sent tears rushing up her throat to fill her eyes. ''I will. Whatever you want, Ben.'' She wasn't used to having someone worry about her.

He looked back at his paperwork, jotting something down with his pencil.

She stood. ''I'll go see Louis the shrink. Everything will work out. I promise.''

''Also, the policemen's banquet is Saturday night.''

''I know.''

''I want you to go.''

''Ben, you know how I feel about those things.''

''I want you to go and I want you to talk to people, to smile, to be nice and to show everyone you're worth having around. You're worth saving. I want you to try and make some friends around here.''

''I have friends,'' she defended, but she knew he wasn't buying.

''I want you to be part of the team. If you're ever

going to make it back, you're going to have to be a team player. Is that clear?"

"Yes, sir," she said resignedly. "I'll be there."

"Good."

She turned toward the door.

"And Willa?"

She stopped. What more could he possibly want?

"Bring a date, and I don't mean Johnny."

She pivoted on her heel. "What's wrong with Johnny?"

"He's your brother and everyone knows it. It's time you start getting along with people and that means finding yourself a date."

A date! Where would she find a date? Jeff's image flashed before her, not the squeaky clean way he looked earlier at the church, but the rugged look he'd had that morning. Chills pimpled her arms, apprehension filled her heart. What if he said no? He wouldn't, she told herself. Would he?

"Do you pay this much attention to everyone's personal life?" she demanded.

Ben's mouth hardened. "Don't you start with me! Now get out of here and go find yourself a date, or you can forget coming back to this precinct, is that clear?"

"Yes, sir. Absolutely and positively." Once more she headed to the door before he could add any more conditions to ruin her life.

"Wait."

She stopped, steeling herself.

"You have to come over for dinner tonight."

Her eyebrows lifted.

"Margo has been worried sick about you and if you don't come over and eat and prove to her you're just fine, I'll have another miserable night listening to her moan and berate me for sending you up that mountain in the first place."

"All right." She sighed. Ben and Margo had been the closest thing to a real family she'd had since her mother died. Even though they could never replace her parents, they had tried and she couldn't help but love them for it. "I'd love to see Margo. Tell her I'll be there in an hour."

Chapter Nine

Willa grunted in disgust at the perky blond newscaster smiling across the TV screen and clicked off the power button. The woman had portrayed her as a complete idiot, implying she'd lured a suspect from an ongoing investigation up to the mountains to terrorize kids from a church group. L.A.'s media goons jumped right on any chance to attack the LAPD.

As if tonight's banquet wasn't going to be tough enough, now she'd have the whole precinct glaring down her back. She ripped off a red sequined dress, threw it over her head to land on a massive pile of discards, and pulled on a small black silk shift. She had to look just right: demure, respectful, sexy and totally capable of enticing a man. Any man, if she so chose. Tonight, the policemen's banquet would be Act One of her hopefully short-lived performance to convince the captain she would play by his rules. Hard-headed as they were.

She cringed as the phone rang and hoped it wasn't

Ben. Hoped by some miracle he missed the news tonight.

"Hey, honey. Just saw you on the news."

Willa let out a relieved breath. "Oh, hi, Margo."

"Don't let that newswoman get you down. It's just part of the job. Are you ready for the party?"

"I guess. I still can't believe Ben is torturing me this way. What does going to parties have to do with being a cop?"

"He just wants you to fit in, honey. Let him help you."

"I don't have a choice," she muttered.

"So, are you going to tell me about your date?"

Willa smiled as the thought of sun-washed hair and dancing blue eyes filled her mind. "He's incredibly handsome and kind and thoughtful." The image of two days' stubble darkening his chin had her feeling loopy. She imagined the short bristles rubbing against her skin and the softness of his lips against hers.... Reeling, she dropped onto the bed and took a deep fortifying breath.

"He sounds wonderful."

"He is. I'll see you later at the party." Willa smiled as she hung up the phone. She had to admit, going to the banquet with Jeff wouldn't be too terribly painful. Thank goodness he accepted her invitation.

She applied a thin layer of makeup. "This isn't a date," she told her reflection. "He's just doing me a favor. Keep that in mind, and no one will get hurt. Especially me." She fluffed her hair and, at the last minute, dabbed on a few dots of her favorite vanilla fragrance.

The doorbell rang.

"It's not a date," she repeated. "Just two friends having dinner." She'd only gone two steps and her heart jump-started a steady beat that grew into an ear-racking pound by the time she reached the door. She took a deep breath and, on impulse, looked through the peephole. A humongous bouquet of flowers blocked her view. Flowers! For her? No one had ever brought her flowers before. Cautiously, she opened the door.

Jeff stood in the hall, a wide smile playing across his face as he held the biggest, most beautiful bouquet of flowers she'd ever seen.

"Oh my," she said, her mouth suddenly going dry. She was staring, standing there with her mouth wide open.

He cleared his throat.

"Oh! Please, come in. I'm sorry. Can I get you anything?"

He smiled and held out the flowers. "These are for you." His eyes caught hers, holding them captive as he handed her the bouquet. A lump balled in her throat. Was it possible he was even more handsome in the light-gray suit than he'd been in jeans and flannel? "You look beautiful tonight."

"Thanks. You, too," she said, and realized how dumb she sounded the moment the words left her mouth. "I mean these are beautiful. I'll go…I'll go put them in water," she said, and quickly escaped into the kitchen. She leaned against the counter and tried to catch her breath.

"Have I mentioned how glad I am you called?" he said as he walked into the room.

She didn't look up, just stood admiring the flowers in her hands, smelling their heady scent, and letting the warmth of his voice swirl around her.

"Me, too," she said softly, and once again felt herself drawn into his gaze as she looked up at him. How was it possible he could have such a strong effect on her?

"Are you ready?"

"Um, sure," she responded. But was she? She'd thought so before he'd walked through the door and sent her world spinning like a child's top across her perfectly ordered life.

"You don't sound sure."

"I don't? I mean, why wouldn't I be? Dancing, dining..." Displaying herself for inspection like a butterfly pinned to black velvet under glass.

"Why do I get the feeling you don't want to go to this shindig tonight?"

"Can't say, really," she said. But she thought, maybe because it's the last place on earth I want to be. Maybe because the only place I really want to be is right here with you. She was getting ahead of herself. He was just a friend, someone who was going to help her convince the captain to let her back on the street. Someone who would show all those cops in the department that she wasn't afraid of people. She could have a relationship. She could trust. Sometimes.

Jeff stepped closer, laid his hands on her shoulders and gave her a gentle squeeze of encouragement.

"You'll be great and you'll have fun. Trust me, you'll see."

"I do trust you. Though I'm not sure why."

"I do. How many other guys have saved your life, thrown you in a river, then made you sleep among bat guano in an authentic bat cave?"

She laughed. "Not a one."

He pulled her close, and if she let herself, she could easily fall against his chest and relish the feel of his heart beating against her own.

"See, there you go." His voice dropped an octave, caressing her soul. "All those other guys, they just don't know how to show a lady a good time. Tonight we're going to eat good food, drink good wine and dance the night away. You'll spend the entire night wrapped in my arms. How much safer can it get than that?"

She felt those arms around her now. The warmth of his body chased away any doubts or fears she might have had. Her knees weakened and she leaned closer. She raised her chin as her eyelids fluttered closed. And this time, he did kiss her. Soft warm lips, just as she'd imagined, claimed her—gently at first, then stronger.

She twined her arms around his neck and pulled him closer to deepen the kiss. She wanted more of him, more of his taste, his warmth. He was intoxicating and he filled an emptiness inside her she hadn't realized existed. Slowly, the kiss ended, but its essence lingered on her lips.

"Mmm." What could she say? Thanks for the incredible kiss? Do we still have to go? Can't we just sit on the couch and kiss some more?

He didn't relinquish his hold, but looked down at her, his soft breath caressing her cheek. "I've wanted to do that since the night I wiped that smudge of dirt off your nose."

Willa smiled, remembering as well. She let her hands slide across his shoulders to rest on his chest.

"Are you ready?" he asked, the rich timbre of his voice stroking her fluttering nerves. She didn't want to move.

"Uh-huh," she answered and hoped the part of her brain that formed words would kick back into gear before they reached the banquet. She picked up her jacket off the chair and let him help her into it. His hands lingered on her arms and it became apparent she wasn't the only one who didn't want to go.

But she had a job to do tonight, a performance to give, and suddenly she didn't think it was going to be all that difficult. After all, she could think of a whole lot worse ways to spend the evening than dancing the night away wrapped in Jeff's arms.

She gave him a playful smile. "Let's go have some fun."

Willa and Jeff walked into the hotel courtyard where round linen-covered tables circled an open-air dance floor. A band, set up in the corner, played soft music. Candlelight flickered through crystal, and tiny white fairy lights twinkled in a tall hedge enclosing the courtyard. "It's almost magical," Willa said.

"What do you mean almost?" Jeff took her around the waist and swung her onto the dance floor. She landed lightly, pivoting on the balls of her feet as he turned her round and round. Before she could become disoriented, he pulled her close to nestle in his arms. Willa laughed and rested her head on his shoulder, a slight smile touching her lips as the warm winds caressed her shoulders. She blew out a deep sigh.

"Better be careful. Someone might think you're actually enjoying yourself."

"Can't have that," she murmured. "What about you? Are you enjoying yourself?"

"How can I not? A smart, funny, beautiful woman calls me up and asks to dance the night away. It doesn't get much better than that."

She smiled. "I bet women call you all the time." It was meant as a casual question, but Willa couldn't help the uneasy expectation washing over her while she waited for his answer.

His smile faltered. "If you're asking me if I date much, the answer is no."

Heat blossomed in her cheeks, while relief stole into her heart.

"I was in a serious relationship a couple of years ago. I thought we had something special. I devoted a lot to her, to us. The distraction took my attention away from Dawn." Pain crossed his features as he stared off above her head.

"Dawn was the girl from your church who was killed?"

He nodded. "I should have been more attentive to my kids."

Willa pulled him a little closer. "What happened with the woman?"

"Apparently I wasn't the man she thought I was."

''I'm sorry. But I'm glad you're here with me.'' She gave him a small smile. ''My captain is a little disillusioned with me, right now. Sometimes we can't be all things to all people. It's that perfection thing—it's hard to master.''

He smiled and gave her a gentle squeeze. ''All anyone has to do is look in your eyes to see what a special person you are. You wear your heart for all to see.''

''Do I?''

Willa smiled as his tender words filled her. No one had ever talked to her like that before. She wasn't quite sure how to respond, but a wise person wouldn't make more out of it than there was. He was a wonderful guy; he said wonderful things. Tonight, she would just enjoy the moment for however long it lasted.

As the song ended, Jeff led her off the dance floor. His steady hand on the small of her back sent delicate little shivers running up her spine. She noticed a crowd forming and abruptly stopped and turned, placing her palms flat against his chest. ''Couldn't we dance just one more?''

He looked down into her eyes, a playful smile lifting the corners of his mouth. ''We could, but I think we're about to have company.''

Willa turned and was instantly swept up into a grand hug from her dearest friend.

''It's so good to see you enjoying yourself,'' Margo said with a squeeze.

''I'm so glad you're here,'' Willa replied, hugging her back. She glanced up at the captain who stood beaming like a Cheshire cat. She bit back the smart retort teetering on the edge of her tongue and pulled Jeff into their little circle. "I'd like you to meet Jeff MacPhearson," she said proudly and with a small note of triumph in her voice. "My date."

"It's wonderful to meet you, Jeff," Margo announced, then turned to Ben with a victorious smile. "See, Ben, I knew Willa would find herself a nice young man, and such a handsome one, too."

Willa grinned. "And Jeff, this is my good friend, Margo, whose kitchen I practically lived in as a child."

Jeff offered her his hand and a friendly smile.

"And the beaming giant behind her is Captain Ben Armstrong, her husband and my boss."

"Great to meet you," Ben boomed and pumped Jeff's hand. "Jeff MacPhearson, that name sounds familiar."

"Now, Ben," Willa admonished. "Surely you saw that woman massacre me on the six o'clock news tonight," she said, getting it out in the open and hopefully over with. "She named Jeff as the unfortunate pastor." Willa straightened, preparing for that look of disapproval he was so good at delivering.

"He did, darling," Margo said. "But he's promised me he won't discuss it this evening. Besides, it wasn't all that bad. And you, my dear, looked fabulous."

Willa had to laugh at that. According to Margo, if you were going to get your face plastered all over the television, it didn't matter much what they said about you as long as you looked fabulous.

"Didn't she, Ben?" Margo insisted.

Willa's lips twitched in amusement at the pained expression crossing Ben's face.

"Now come," Margo interjected. "Let's go inside and get a table, I'm starving and I want to hear all about how you and Jeff got on up there in the mountains with all those kids."

"Well that, I'd say, is obvious, dear," Ben mumbled. Willa caught Jeff's grin before Margo linked their arms and led them through the row of French doors and into the main dining room.

Jeff followed close behind them, watching as Willa conversed happily with Margo. Once again she'd become the woman he'd met on the mountain, completely at ease with herself—funny, brilliant and shining. It was clear she didn't feel comfortable among her colleagues and he'd guess from the looks they threw her way that the feeling was mutual.

While the tables filled around them, the two seats available at theirs remained empty. Was it because of Ben or Willa that people kept walking by? The thought saddened him. Here was a beautiful, vivacious woman, yet she didn't seem to have any friends.

Except for Margo.

From the content expression on Ben's face as he watched the two women talk, it was obvious how much he loved them. And from what he could see, Willa deserved it. She was warmhearted, kind, sweet, and his body was still reeling from their kiss.

He still couldn't believe he kissed her. He couldn't even imagine what had possessed him to do so. One minute he was standing there and the next thing he knew she was in his arms, tangling up his insides. He didn't even know he could kiss like that, with such total abandon. He'd lost complete use of his senses, and it was intense. Beyond intense. And if he wasn't careful, he could lose a lot more than his senses. That wasn't something he could afford right now.

He didn't know if she was "the one." As much as he admired and cared for her, he knew she'd be just as uncomfortable in his world as she appeared to be in her own. Though she had warmed up to his kids. They even liked and admired her as much as he did. But he wasn't sure how she'd stand up to the scrutiny of their parents. Then again, she was an enigma and totally unpredictable. He had a sneaky suspicion she just might surprise him.

"May we join you?" An older man and his wife stood behind the two unoccupied chairs.

"Yes, of course, please." Jeff stood, while the two sat. He'd recognized the man instantly from his work two years before at Sun Valley church.

"Pete, Ann, how have you been?" Ben asked.

"Good," Pete replied, while Ann just nodded. They both sat, and placed their napkins in their laps.

"Pete O'Donnelly, isn't it?" Jeff asked.

"Yes." Pete scrutinized him for a moment before recognition took hold. "Why, Pastor MacPhearson. It's been a long time. How have you been?" Pete offered his hand.

"Very well, thanks."

"Heard you moved to Pasadena."

Servers efficiently placed plates of roast beef swimming in gravy with all the trimmings before them.

"Yep, about two years, now."

Pete cut into his meat, his expression thoughtful. "Pretty up there."

"Yeah," Jeff replied, and started on his beef. What could he say? It *was* prettier and cleaner and safer. It was utopia compared to the parish where he'd first met Officer Pete O'Donnelly. And the circumstances he'd met him under. He stole a glance at Willa, but she was deep in a conversation with Margo.

"That program you started," Pete said in between bites, "helping the kids. It's doing real well."

"Really?" Jeff asked with interest, though he wasn't sure why he was surprised. Just because he'd given up, didn't mean the others had, too.

"Oh, yes. They've made a lot of progress. They even have a shelter where a lot of the kids can live until they get their heads screwed on straight. Of course, there are those who never do and end up back on the street, and a couple have even ended up like that Dawn kid."

Just the mention of her named poked a sore spot that would probably never heal. The child who got away. The lost one he couldn't help.

"But they've had their success stories, too. You should stop by and check it out. You have a lot to be proud of."

Jeff smiled, overcome with bittersweet pride. "Thank you, I think I will." He stared into his coffee cup, realizing that for the first time in two years, the thought of going back to Sun Valley didn't send anxiety surging through him. In fact, he was interested in the progress they'd made, and the hurdles they'd had to overcome.

"Been doing similar stuff up there where you are?" Pete asked casually.

"I'm still working with kids," Jeff replied, knowing full well it didn't even come close. "Still trying to help them grow up," he offered with a smile.

"Well, if they're anything like our son, they never do," Pete joked.

"Willa, we saw you on the news tonight," Ann said.

Jeff sensed Willa stiffening beside him.

"Didn't she look fabulous?" Margo cut in before Willa could reply.

"Made the whole department look good, as usual," Pete grumbled.

Ben pointed with his fork. "Pete, you know the media, they're always blowing things out of proportion."

Pete nodded. "That's true. I've been on the news a few times myself."

"You and me, both," Ben added.

An easy banter started and everyone at the table participated. Everyone except Willa. Jeff had seen the newscast, too. And while it hadn't portrayed her in the best light, she certainly hadn't looked incompetent. "The dancing has started on the patio again," he whispered in her ear. "Would you like to join me?" The grateful look in her large green eyes set his heart skipping a beat.

"I'd love to," she answered and graced him with a smile that almost had him forgetting they were surrounded by hundreds of people, almost had him pulling her into his arms and losing himself in her kiss. Almost.

Instead he settled for holding her close, enjoying her warmth against his chest, her soft curves against his hands, and her sweet scent of vanilla and cream. They had the floor to themselves as they swayed to the enchanting music. "What made you decide to become a cop?" he asked, curious why she'd stay in a position she seemed so uncomfortable in.

"I was a lost and confused teenager, and not sure what I wanted to do. My older brother, Johnny, followed in my father's footsteps and went into law enforcement. It seemed to work for him, so I joined the academy, too."

"Do you like it?"

"Like it?"

"Yeah, are you happy?"

She looked confused for a second. "Yes. I mean there are good days and bad days, but overall I think I'm good at what I do, and I think I make a difference, small as it is, trying to keep the streets safe."

"Do you have a partner?"

"Why do you ask?"

"Curious, I guess. Don't all cops have partners?"

"Not me. I like to work alone."

"Why's that? I'd think you'd want someone to bounce ideas off of, to—"

"Partners make a cop reckless. They let their defenses down because they think they have backup. They rely on that person when things get tough, setting themselves up for a fall. That person might not always be there, and if he's not, you're dead."

"Did that happen to you? Did someone rely on

you? Is that why you're so uncomfortable with these people?''

Willa stopped dancing, shock hardening her eyes. ''No, of course not. I'm not uncomfortable.''

''You're not?''

''No. What makes you think I'm uncomfortable? I'm here, aren't I? I'm dancing, laughing, having a grand ole time. I'm not uncomfortable.''

He raised his arms, palms up in a defensive posture. ''Okay, okay.''

She pulled his arms down, but kept his hands clasped within her own. ''A lot of these people don't like my methods,'' she confessed. ''Ben complains that I'm not a team player and that some of the cops don't feel I'll back them up.''

''Is he right?'' He knew he shouldn't ask, it was too soon, too personal, but maybe he could help her if he could get her to talk about it.

''No...maybe. They can count on me. I don't feel I can count on them.''

''Why not?''

''Ben was my father's partner. They were out on a call—my father was killed. It wasn't Ben's fault. I realize that. There's only one person to blame for my dad's death, and that's Jack Paulson. But he got off. The others think I'm on a vendetta, that I'll do whatever it takes to bring Jack down...and they're absolutely right.''

The bitterness in her voice overwhelmed him. ''I see.''

''What do you see? Do you agree with them?''

Her eyes hardened again. Why was she so quick to assume he was thinking the worst? He pulled her close. ‘‘Willa, I think you’re a great cop and if you can take care of Jack and keep Tracey and other lost children safe, then you’re more than great. You’re awesome.’’

A tremulous smile crossed her lips. ‘‘Thank you.’’

‘‘I also believe it’s important that you focus on what really matters.’’

‘‘And that is…?’’

‘‘Keeping this city safe, protecting the innocents, doing good because it makes *you* feel good, it makes *you* proud of who you are and what you’re able to accomplish. Leaving your mark on the world, so you know when you leave this place that you’ve made a difference, you’ve made it better.’’

‘‘That’s a lot to live up to,’’ Willa replied softly.

‘‘Not really. You’re almost there.’’

‘‘Almost?’’ she challenged.

‘‘If you let your motives slip into a grudge or a vendetta, then you’re coming at it from a dark place. Your goal isn’t to do good, it’s to cause destruction.’’

‘‘It’s to right a wrong and there’s nothing bad about that.’’

He held her tighter, but she was no longer soft and pliable, she was stiff with her chin raised and a fire burning deep in her eyes.

‘‘You sound like all the rest,’’ she said.

‘‘But I’m not like all the rest.’’

‘‘What’s the difference?’’

‘‘The difference is, I believe in you.’’ To his surprise, tears misted her angry eyes. He pulled her back into his arms. At first she resisted, but then she rested her head on his shoulder and they swayed in silence for the remainder of the song.

Chapter Ten

"Mind if I cut in?" Ben asked, catching Willa off guard. She hadn't danced with Ben in years, not since he'd taken her to the father-daughter dance in high school. She stepped into his embrace. He didn't seem so big to her now, nor did she feel so clumsy.

"You look beautiful tonight," he said, smiling down at her.

"Thank you," Willa replied, pleased, though it irked her to admit it. They'd been at odds for so long, she wasn't sure she liked getting compliments from him. "Aren't you afraid what this will look like to the rest of the department?" She'd noticed the stares of several of her fellow officers as they danced across the floor.

"Nope."

"Why's that?"

"Because you're family, Willa. And family comes first, always."

His words tightened her throat. ''Stop it.''

''Why?''

''Because you're going to make me cry.''

Ben laughed, deep and loud. ''Well, we can't have that now, can we? It would shatter that tough-woman image you've worked so hard to maintain.''

''Yes, it would.'' She smiled, and began to relax.

''You look happy.''

''I guess I am.''

''Jeff have anything to do with that?''

She glanced at Jeff as he moved Margo expertly across the floor. Taking in his easy smile and confident grace, how could she not be drawn to him? ''I suppose it does. He's a pretty special guy.''

''I can see that.''

''Too special for me, though,'' she muttered under her breath.

Ben caught her chin, pulling her gaze back to him. ''Now, what's that supposed to mean?''

''Come on, Ben. He's a pastor. His whole life is devoted to God and helping children. Do you see someone like me fitting into that picture?''

''I see you fitting in very well. You're a wonderful person, Willa, with a generous heart. You've just let yourself get a little off track the last few years.''

''Have not,'' she defended.

''It's my fault. I never should have let you work Jack's territory.''

''Ben! There's nothing wrong with me. Nothing for you to take blame for. I'm committed to bringing Jack to justice for what he did to my dad. Would someone please tell me what's so wrong with that?''

"Nothing, Willa. Nothing's wrong with that, as long as you don't give up your entire life to do it. You have a chance here with this guy. And he's good, Willa, someone your father would have been proud to see you with."

"My father can never be proud until his killer is punished."

Ben's grip tightened on her waist. "How could you think that? Your father loved you. He would be proud of the person you are."

"Ben, I—"

"You could have become a teacher, a nurse or a waitress and he still would have been proud of you. You didn't have to become a cop and you certainly don't have to catch his killer to make him proud. Wherever he is, he is proud of the good person you are right now."

"I hear what you're saying, Ben."

"Do you? I hope so, because if you put half the energy and passion into making this thing with Jeff work as you've put into nabbing Jack, you two could have something really special. Something like me and Margo."

Willa smiled. She couldn't disagree with him. Ben and Margo were the happiest couple she'd ever met. Soul mates, her mom had always said. Ben's grip loosened.

"There's a better way to honor his memory, Willa. Be happy, that's all he ever wanted for you. That's all any of us want for you."

"Okay, Ben." She couldn't argue with him. There

was a catch in the back of her throat, and tears were burning the back of her eyes. ''I'm sorry for causing you so much trouble.''

''Don't be sorry, just promise me you'll think about what I've said, and you'll give this young man of yours a chance.''

''I will, but you're jumping the gun a little bit here. This is only our first date.''

''Hogwash. I've seen the way he looks at you. He can't take his eyes off you and he has that same puppy-dog stare I used to get every time I saw Margo.''

Willa laughed. ''He does not.'' Once more, she searched the dance floor, and when she found Jeff his gaze was on her as if he hadn't let her out of his sight.

''Ridiculous,'' she muttered.

''You're worth it,'' Ben said softly.

As the song ended, he handed her over to Jeff and reclaimed his wife. Willa moved easily back into Jeff's arms. A perfect fit, she thought, then chided herself. She was letting Ben get to her. Jeff was not her soul mate. As if there was such a thing.

''Margo is such a riot,'' Jeff said, laughing. ''And boy, does she love you.''

''Oh, no. Don't tell me she was boring you with tales from my childhood.''

''Only the most embarrassing moments.'' Smile lines creased his eyes.

''Please, spare me the rehash.'' Willa's mind raced trying to imagine what Margo could have said.

He laughed. ''Now, what fun would that be?''

''Okay, that's my cue to find the ladies' room. Can I trust you while I'm gone? Or are you going to dig up some of my more colorful secrets?''

''Hmm, that I just might do.''

Willa rolled her eyes and left in search of the rest room. Could he really want to be with her? She smiled at the possibilities. As she passed a gigantic palm at the edge of the room, she heard two voices discussing Jack. She stopped in her tracks and pretended to dig in her purse for change for the telephone. She peeked through the long spindly leaves, trying to get a good look at the men talking.

''Yeah, Jack's set up new digs. It won't take him long before he's back in business,'' Rick Masters, one of the cops who'd picked her up in front of Jack's apartment building, said. ''I really thought Willa had the goods on him this time. I should have known better.''

Willa's stomach clenched at his words.

''Don't be so hard on her, she's gotten closer to him than anyone else has managed to do,'' his partner, Cliff, replied.

You got that right, she thought.

''Not anymore, not if the captain has anything to do with it,'' Rick responded. ''She came too close to biting it this time for him to deal with. I bet she spends the rest of her career pushing paper behind some desk.''

''Not if I have anything to say about it,'' she muttered under her breath.

''Yeah, what a shame,'' Cliff said. ''We won't get

to see her strutting her stuff in those skintight little outfits anymore.''

''Yeah, she was looking real hot—''

''All right, that's enough,'' Willa said, bursting through the plant.

''Eavesdropping? How juvenile. Even for you,'' Cliff taunted.

The urge to slap that sarcastic gleam right out of his eye was almost overwhelming, but as tempting as the thought was, she couldn't afford to mess up the good-girl image she had worked so hard to sustain all night. ''What's this about Jack?''

''What's it to you?'' Cliff asked.

''Yeah, you're off the case, banished,'' his chubby buddy said, enjoying himself way too much.

''Give it to me,'' she demanded.

''And have the captain jumping down my throat? I don't think so. There is no way I'm going to put his little Willa in jeopardy. We all saw how close you two are tonight,'' Rick said.

''Yeah, a little too close, if you ask me,'' Cliff replied. The men knocked their bottles together in mutual agreement.

Willa fumed. ''No one *is* asking you. And no one is keeping me off Jack's back. Tell me what you know. Now. Or I'll find a way to make you regret it.''

''Go ahead.'' Cliff nodded to his partner. ''Tell her. It's her butt, not yours. Maybe this time the captain will kick her completely out of the department.''

''In your dreams,'' Willa growled. ''Now spill.''

''Fine. He's set up shop over on K Street in the

warehouse district,'' Rick answered. ''Your buddy Carlos is there, too.''

Willa cringed at the mention of Carlos's name. ''Any girls?''

''Didn't see any.''

''Anyone got him staked?''

''What for? He hasn't done anything.''

''Carlos kidnapped a thirteen-year-old girl,'' Willa snapped in disbelief.

''Says who?'' Cliff challenged. ''The girl hasn't been in to give her statement.''

''She hasn't?'' An uneasy feeling gnawed at her. Why hadn't Tracey's mother brought her in yet?

''Nope, and no one can seem to locate her. Any idea where she's holed up? 'Cause now Carlos is going to have two reasons to go after her. One, to save Jack's butt, and the other, to save his own.''

Willa nodded in agreement. Tracey's mother should have gotten settled into a safe place and called her by now. She hoped the woman didn't think she could just ignore the situation. She had to bring Tracey in for a statement. It was the only way to protect the girl.

''In fact, you'd better watch your own tail,'' Rick added.

''I certainly won't count on you to do it.''

''Sweet thing, I've always got your tail in sight.''

''You two are pathetic,'' Willa groaned, and walked away. What was Jack up to? If only she could get back to the strip and find out what the word was on the street, but she doubted any of the girls would talk to her now that her cover was blown. They probably felt betrayed and used. Perhaps she could get Jeff to drive down K Street and check out Jack's new place on the way back to her apartment.

A warehouse. What would Jack want with a warehouse?

Willa stared out the window as the freeway exit signs whipped by. Two more miles and they'd reach the K Street exit. She had to think of a way to get Jeff to take the exit without broaching the subject of Jack again. Especially since he'd been going on for the past ten minutes about the wonderful time he'd had. And it had been wonderful, she mused, especially when they'd been dancing.

Pushing the thought aside, she shifted in her seat. Perhaps she could ask if he'd ever been to that new Chinese place everyone had been talking about, the one on K Street. No, that wouldn't work. There's no way he could be hungry after that huge dinner. A bar? No. She doubted the good pastor frequented bars in slumville.

She could see the sign now, K Street exit, one mile ahead.

"Well?" Jeff asked, breaking into her thoughts.

"Huh?" She hadn't heard a word he'd said. "I'm sorry, what were you saying?" she asked as the K Street exit zoomed by.

"I was wondering if you'd come to my service tomorrow morning."

"Service? Like in church?"

"Yes."

Cold dread gripped her heart. "Oh, I don't think I've ever felt comfortable in a church."

''How many times have you been?'' he pressed.

Willa racked her brain. How many times had she been? ''I'm not sure.''

''Is it the hard benches? The music? The drive?''

''No. Um...I don't know. I guess I don't like the feeling that someone's watching me.''

Jeff smiled, his shoulders shaking with a silent chuckle.

''Don't laugh. The concept of the ever watchful deity just doesn't sit well with me.''

''Watchful, not judgmental,'' he reminded her.

''Of course He's judgmental. If He doesn't pass judgment, how can scum like Jack and Carlos get their just desserts? Don't tell me they'll be sitting up there on a cloud and I'll have to look at their ugly mugs for all eternity. Don't even go there.''

Jeff didn't respond, just expertly maneuvered the car down L.A.'s monstrous freeways.

''What?'' she demanded. Even his soundless chuckles were better than nothing.

''I'm still trying to absorb your concept of heaven.''

''Well? If He doesn't judge, how are the bad, and I mean the *really* bad, punished?''

''They've turned their backs on God, they will never sit in His grace. How much worse can it get than that?''

''A lot. They should burn in the eternal fire with little pitchforks poking their eyes.''

Finally, he laughed, and the sound of its deep warmth swelled inside her.

''Are we feeling a little hostility?''

''Maybe,'' she paused. ''Just a little.''

"Willa, God is always there for you. If you still your heart and listen, He'll tell you what you should do, which path you should follow. He'll help you find your way."

"I didn't know I was lost."

"Jack and Carlos lead dark lives now and they'll lead dark lives in the hereafter, you can count on that." He placed a hand on her knee and squeezed for emphasis. "Don't let them consume you. Focus on the good in your life."

"I am. Tonight was good." She'd gotten a lead on Jack and, as soon as Tracey's mom called, she'd bring Tracey in to give a statement and get the Jack-ball rolling. "I'm sorry, Jeff. But passivity is not in my makeup. I believe in an eye for an eye, not turning the other cheek. I can never be the kind of woman you want or need, because the streets are always going to be a major part of my life."

"At the expense of everything else?"

"If it comes to that." Her words hung between them.

"How is it you know what kind of woman I want or need?"

She looked at him, surprised. "I guess I don't. I just assumed it wouldn't be someone like me."

"You mean someone fun, warm and beautiful?"

She stared at him. *Is that really how he saw her?*

"Perhaps you don't know *me* very well. Perhaps we need a little more time to get to know one another better." Jeff pulled into her complex and parked the car. He turned off the ignition, swiveled in his seat, and looked at her intently.

Willa bit her lip.

"We have something here," he continued. "I can feel it and you can, too. It's stronger than the two of us apart. Are you going to deny we have a connection?"

"No, of course not." How could she? Even now she longed to snuggle close to his chest and feel his arms wrap around her. "I don't know what to say. I'm afraid I'm not very good at this dating stuff."

"Say you'll come to the barbecue with me at the church tomorrow evening and you'll give what we have going here a chance."

How could she say no to that? Especially when every molecule of her being wanted to climb into his pocket and never leave. But would she lose her edge? Would she become all soft and mushy and goo-goo eyed? How would that affect her the next time Carlos caught her off guard? Would she have it in her to escape him?

Jeff pulled her into his arms. He was comforting and warm and his spicy aftershave filled her as she inhaled. She took a deep breath as if breathing alone would bring him closer. Would she want to give up this—give up him—just to keep her edge?

He rubbed his thumb along her jaw, softly caressing her skin. "You are the most beautiful woman I've ever met," he whispered.

And she knew he was going to kiss her again, hoped he'd kiss her again and again. She moistened her lips and lost herself in his gaze as he moved closer and closer.

"Jeff," she whispered as his lips closed over hers—

soft, sweet, and entrancing. She fell, plummeting, clutching his shoulders as if they were her last hold on the world as she knew it. How could she not do whatever he asked? She couldn't think, couldn't feel, couldn't see or hear. All she could do was hang on tight and lose herself in his embrace.

"Oh, Jeff," she murmured.

"I'm here for you, Willa," Jeff murmured. He pulled away, and she leaned her head on his shoulder.

"I suppose I'll have to go to the barbecue with you now." She sighed. For another kiss like that, she was certain she'd go to the end of the earth.

"Good." He paused a minute then said, "I'm considering visiting my old parish in the morning."

"Really?"

"Yeah. Officer Pete O'Donnelly piqued my curiosity about the shelter and the kids they're helping. Would you come with me?"

The hope in his voice surprised her. "Are you nervous about going back there again?"

"No. It's just been a while, and I left so quickly after Dawn's death."

"Jeff, what happened to Dawn wasn't your fault. You're being too hard on yourself. Even if you had said all the wrong words or spent more time with a friend than you had with her, it still wouldn't have been your fault. She was a runaway, a mixed-up kid who got lost and was taken advantage of by some very bad people."

"I know, but—"

"You can blame yourself, you can blame her parents, you can blame God, but all that blaming won't bring her back. And it won't make you feel better. All you can do is your best to help other kids and hope it doesn't happen again.'' She rested her hand on his cheek. ''It's okay to forgive yourself.''

He placed his hands over hers and closed his eyes. ''I wish it were that simple.''

She smiled. ''Me, too. But I think going back to Sun Valley is a great way to start. How about a cup of coffee before your drive back to Pasadena?''

''Sure.'' They got out of the car and walked hand in hand toward the stairs to her second-floor apartment.

''Maybe there will be someone at the shelter who can give us a line on Jack. You know, one of the runaways?''

Jeff laughed. ''You are relentless.''

''That's what they say.'' Willa unlocked the door and they walked in. The first thing she noticed was the blinking red light on her answering machine. The second was the smell.

Chapter Eleven

Willa recognized the smell the moment she walked through the door. "Do you smell cigarettes?"

"A little, but there's something else." Jeff walked farther into the room. "I can't put my finger on it."

Willa crossed to the phone and hit the play button on her answering machine. Evelyn Wilcox's voice filled the room, explaining how she and Tracey were out of town visiting a relative and that they'd be returning around 3:00 p.m. tomorrow.

"You can reach us at the Montague Hotel on Cordova Street in Pasadena." She took a deep steadying breath. "Tracey and I are ready for her to give her statement." She hung up without saying goodbye.

"She sounds scared," Jeff said, concern filling his eyes.

"True. But she also sounds under control. She's aware of what they have to face, and they've taken the time to prepare for it." Willa gave his arm a comforting pat. "They'll be okay. They're dealing with this together."

Jeff nodded. "You're right. The hard part for Tracey was confronting her mom and telling her what she was feeling. It sounds like they have that behind them now."

"Being a single parent is tough. Believe me, my mother and I had some major issues before she died," Willa said absently as she circled the room.

"How'd she die?"

Willa stopped. "It was right after I finished high school. Car accident."

"I'm sorry."

"Thanks. It's okay. It's been a while now." And she did better when she didn't think about how much she wished things had been different between them. She wrinkled her nose. She still couldn't get the smell of cigarette smoke out of her mind. Had someone been in her apartment while she'd been gone? The notion left her edgy and uncomfortable. This was her private space. Here, she wasn't Blondie and she wasn't Officer Barrett, she was just Willa. Somehow that felt violated, but she had nothing to go on, just an uncomfortable twinge in her gut.

She strode to her bedroom and pulled open the top drawer in her nightstand. Her Beretta was still lying where she'd left it, right beside the paperback she'd been reading. Snatching up the gun, she held it against her chest, then blew out a deep sigh of relief, feeling immensely better. If a thief had been in her apartment tonight, he would have easily found her gun and taken it.

Jeff stood in the doorway, his eyes wide with surprise as he watched her.

"It's still here," she breathed.

"I hadn't even considered..." Slowly, he moved into the room. "A gun."

"Well, I am a cop," she said, and felt a little absurd. Of course she had a gun.

"I guess I expected you to have something... smaller."

Willa lifted it up and down, weighing it. "It's not too bad, not really. Not compared to a lot of others out there."

"I suppose not."

"Wanna hold it?" She felt a mischievous smirk lift the corners of her mouth.

He stepped forward, moving into her personal space and staring directly into her eyes. The intensity of his gaze started her heart beating in an uneasy rhythm.

"I don't think so," he whispered. The deep sound of his voice sent echoes reverberating down her spine.

"It's a shame..." she started.

"Yes?"

She forgot what she was going to say. Did he have to stand so close? She took a step back, but her calves butted up against her nightstand. She broke eye contact and tried to shake the fuzzies out of her mind. "It's a shame we live in a world where people feel they have to arm themselves, but the cold, hard truth is that we do."

"True." He removed the gun from her grasp and dropped it back into the drawer.

Why couldn't her heartbeat slow down? Good grief, she felt as if she were going to have a heart attack.

Air, she needed air that wasn't permeated with mint mouthwash, aftershave, and *man.* She stepped out from behind him and out of sheer nervousness began systematically checking the windows throughout the apartment along with the lock on the front door.

A faintly amused expression crossed Jeff's face. "What are you looking for?"

"Any sign of forced entry. I can't get that smell out of my mind or the idea that someone could have been here while we were at the banquet," she answered matter-of-factly. He might believe he was getting to her, but no reason why she needed to make him sure of it.

Jeff helped her examine the locks and do a complete sweep of the apartment before checking the bedroom. "Just to make sure no one is waiting to surprise you while you're sleeping," he added.

"Gee, thanks. But don't forget—" she tilted her head toward the nightstand "—I've been taking care of myself for a long time now." And she certainly didn't need a man to make sure everything was all right.

"Your bedroom window is open."

"It is?" Dubious images shook her bravado. "How far?"

"An inch or two."

"Oh," she said, releasing the breath she'd been holding. "That was my doing. I like the fresh air at night when I sleep. And it is a safe neighborhood," she added to appease the doubtful look he gave her.

"Now that the news media has announced to the world who you are, do me a favor and sleep with your window closed, or at least buy a stick and jam it so it can't be opened any farther.''

''Yes, sir,'' she mocked with a salute. But she hated to admit he was right. Her anonymity was gone thanks to the all-invasive news media. ''I think we're okay, but just to be on the safe side, I'll be waiting at the Montague when Tracey and her mom arrive. If Carlos had been here and heard the call…''

''Do you honestly think he was?''

''Probably not, but why take the chance?''

''All right. After we leave the shelter, we'll grab a bite to eat, then head straight to the hotel.''

''Sounds good. Still want that cup of coffee?''

He reached out and took her hand. ''No, thanks. It's been a long night. Try to get some sleep, okay?''

''I will,'' she agreed, and braced herself to be swept off her feet.

Instead he bent down and kissed her chastely on the cheek, and then, much to her disappointment, left.

A little after noon the next day, Willa dabbed on a bit of lipstick, wrinkled her nose at a funky smell she couldn't seem to find the source of, then joined Jeff in the kitchen. He was sitting at her table, reading the Sunday paper and drinking a cup of hazelnut coffee.

Silently, Willa watched him. She knew how important going back to Sun Valley was to him, to see his old friends and how much things had changed. She hoped it would work out for him and give him some closure. As she knew, some memories were harder to face than others.

He must have felt her staring, for he lowered the paper and met her gaze. Color suffused her cheeks.

‘‘How was your service this morning?’’ she asked, the image of him at the pulpit stealing its way to the forefront of her mind. She realized she wouldn’t mind watching him lead a service. In fact, she was quite curious about what he’d have to say, and how he’d say it. She imagined he could be a very passionate and persuasive speaker.

‘‘Good. You missed out. We talked about hope and family unity.’’

She plastered a look of regret on her face. ‘‘Sounds good. Perhaps next time.’’

Jeff smiled. ‘‘You wait. I foresee you becoming so involved with the church, you’ll be heading the choir one day.’’

Willa choked on her coffee and grimaced as the hot liquid burned her throat. ‘‘Obviously you’ve *never* heard me sing or you wouldn’t suggest such a thing. The very idea makes me sick to my stomach. I think I’d rather have a root canal or maybe even an appendectomy, a slug in the gut—’’

Jeff laughed, loud and hearty. ‘‘Okay, okay. I get the picture. I was only teasing.’’

‘‘And it’s a good thing, too,’’ she said smiling. She was pleased she’d been able to make him laugh. She liked it when he laughed. ‘‘Now let’s get going, I can’t wait to see this creation of yours.’’

Jeff stood and folded the newspaper. Her words struck a sensitive chord within him. ‘‘I wouldn’t call it a creation exactly.’’

‘‘Don’t be silly.’’ Willa locked the door behind them as they left. ‘‘Do you think the place has changed a lot?’’

‘‘Sounds like it. And all for the better, too.’’ He

started the car and as they drove he tried to sort out exactly how he felt about going back. Nervous? Excited? Concerned about how they'd greet him. Perhaps he should have called first and given them a chance to turn him down.

"It will be nice to see everyone again," Willa prompted.

"Yeah," he replied. He hoped it would.

"Have you kept in touch?"

"Not really. My leaving was very sudden."

"Well, I'm sure they'll be happy to see you."

"You think?"

"Of course. Why wouldn't they? You're The Man."

Jeff smiled and relaxed. "That's me. I'm the man." He drove on in silence for a few minutes, then while stopped at a red light, turned to look at her. "How do you do that?"

"Do what?"

"Make everything seem okay."

"Isn't it?"

"And you make me laugh."

"I guess I'm naturally talented."

He gave her a wink. When she was spunky like this, she was just adorable.

"Everything is going to be fine, Jeff. Whatever bad stuff we're dealing with today will be forgotten and pushed aside by whatever bad stuff comes along tomorrow. Don't let today's junk get you down."

He tried to process the jumble of words she'd just spoken. "Is that a Willa mantra?"

"I try to stay focused on what it is I want, and let

everything else roll. The hard part is figuring out what you want.''

''Good advice. Now how do I get you to stay focused on me?''

Willa's smile lit up her whole face. ''How could I not?''

Smiling back, Jeff pulled into the Sun Valley parking lot. He took a deep breath. The lighthearted mood had passed. ''This is it.''

''Doesn't look so intimidating. Inviting even, in a homey kind of way.''

''Good. That's the way it should be. Especially to kids.''

''If I was a kid, I'd definitely feel invited.''

Jeff clasped her hand in his and brought it to his lips. ''Thanks for coming with me.''

''Come on,'' she urged, smiling. ''Let's go in.''

He grasped onto her enthusiasm as they walked into the building. They passed through a small waiting area and proceeded toward an open door halfway down the hall. Jeff poked his head through the doorway. Mike Kelly sat behind a desk two sizes too small for him. ''Still haven't got yourself a desk that fits you?'' Jeff asked and was instantly filled with pleasure at the sight of his old friend.

Mike looked up startled. ''Well, I'll be.'' He dropped his pen and stood, a wide smile brightening his face. ''Jeff, it's so good to see you.'' He came around the desk and enthusiastically shook Jeff's hand. ''How have you been? It's been way too long.''

''That it has,'' Jeff agreed. ''Pastor Mike, I'd like you to meet a good friend of mine, Miss Willa Barrett.''

Mike's large hand encompassed hers. "It's wonderful to meet you, Miss Barrett."

Willa smiled. "You, too."

"Well, come on. Let me show you what we've done to the old place." He led them out of the room and down the hallway to a door at the end, which opened into a large hall.

"This is our fellowship hall where we have lunches, dinners, rummage sales, community activities, and where the homeless sleep on Tuesday nights."

"Really?" Jeff said, impressed. "That's new."

"We started the program about a year ago during the winter months. Now we offer it year-round, though we don't get too many people during the summer, mostly just families looking for someplace safe to sleep. All the churches in the area take them in one night a week. We even have a doctor in our congregation who stops by and looks at those who need it. It's been a wonderful program to watch grow."

"Sounds amazing," Willa said. "Do you keep them separated from the teens that live here?"

"Absolutely. It was a tight fit at first, but we were able to purchase the house behind us and refurbish it for the teen shelter."

"That's great," Jeff said, remembering their concerns over space. They followed him out a back door and across a worn basketball court to a small house built in the forties behind the church. "It was a wreck when we got it, thank goodness, otherwise we wouldn't have been able to raise enough funds to buy it."

They walked across a front yard of dried weeds and up onto the cleanly swept front porch. "We're doing a special fund-raiser next weekend to raise the money to fix up the yards and put in a small picket fence. The kids are doing all the work themselves. They've taken a lot of pride in their house, shopping at local thrift stores for curtains and such.''

As they entered through the front door, Jeff's first thought was how neat and clean everything was. How homey it felt, especially with the smell of baking chocolate wafting through the house.

''Jeff?'' a boy watching T.V. said, and quickly got to his feet.

Delight filled Jeff at the sight of the teen. ''Hey, Jeremy.'' He stepped forward and shook the boy's hand. ''Look at you, all grown up.''

The boy smiled shyly. ''Where you been so long?''

Guilt clenched in Jeff's chest as he dreaded the questions he knew would come and the answers that just weren't good enough.

''Pasadena. Up with my dad.''

''Oh, yeah.'' The boy nodded. ''Heard that.''

''You still shooting those hoops?'' Jeff asked, hoping for more solid ground.

''Every day!''

''Good, keep it up.'' Jeff patted him on the back and continued on their tour. The house had only three bedrooms but the teens used every bit of space it had.

''How many kids stay here?'' Willa asked.

''Right now, there is only room for nine girls. We have six boys living back in an area off the fellowship hall.''

''That's incredible,'' Jeff said. ''There were only three when I left. And to tell the truth, I wasn't sure they were even going to stay.''

"They didn't," Mike said. "After you left and what happened to Dawn, the program just sort of fell apart."

Mike's words felt like a blow to the stomach. After he left… After he failed to save Dawn.

Willa moved closer and took his hand in her own.

He gave it a squeeze.

"But eventually they made their way back," Mike continued. "Mostly in the winter when they'd heard they could sleep here. They were all homeless, without hope, without options. Now they have part-time jobs, a little schooling and a chance for a good future."

Willa noticed a girl she'd seen on the strip while undercover as Blondie. Only now, she wore sweatpants instead of a mini and her face was scrubbed clean. She was smiling and talking companionably with some of the other girls. She'd escaped the streets and from the looks of it, she'd be all right. Thanks to people like Jeff and Mike. A burning sense of pride rushed through her. "How do you get the kids to come here?"

"We send out canvassing teams to talk to them, to let them know we're here for them, no strings attached. We don't ask anything from them in return except that they live clean, healthy lives while they're here. If they make their way into our church and into God's light, that's an added bonus, but our main focus is to save their lives first. We'll worry about their souls later."

Willa smiled. Now this was a practical and pragmatic man. They left the house and stopped on the basketball court where weeds popped up through the aging asphalt. "From what I've seen, I'd say you've been very successful."

"Thanks to Jeff's inspiration," Mike stated.

"No," Jeff denied. "Please don't give any thanks to me. My leaving almost destroyed everything. I left these kids when they needed me the most. I will never be able to forget that. And neither will they."

"Don't be absurd," Mike insisted. "It was your vision and hard work that got the program started. That's what the kids and everyone else won't forget. You said if we could just reach a couple of them, then they'll help us reach the rest, and you were right. It's the kids themselves who convince the ones living on the streets that there is a better alternative, they don't have to lose it all for a sense of freedom, there is someone out there who cares about them."

Willa squeezed Jeff's hand. "I'm very impressed with all the work you've *both* done."

"It's been a long hard road but thanks to the commitment of hardworking people willing to make a difference and a few corporate sponsors, we've been able to pull it off. I hope in the future we'll be able to count on *your* help, Miss Barrett."

"Absolutely," Willa agreed. "Though I must admit, I'm not sure what I could offer."

"God always finds a way to help those who are willing to help us. I have faith in Him, Miss Barrett."

Willa smiled. "Then I do, too. If there's ever a way I can help you, I will."

"How many of the kids are attending services?" Jeff asked softly. The crestfallen look on his face broke her heart. She wished he could see how wonderful he was, and not be so hard on himself.

"Only about a quarter of them at this time. We really need to separate the kids from the rest of the congregation and have a more informal contemporary service for them. I'm afraid dressing up and sitting with a bunch of adults for an hour is a little too overwhelming for a lot of them right now. They're still feeling very insecure about themselves and their futures."

Jeff nodded. "Understandable."

"I obviously don't have the time to take that project on, so we're looking for a youth minister, someone the kids will be able to trust." Mike looked to Jeff. "The job is yours if you want it."

Willa could have sworn she heard Jeff's jaw bounce off the asphalt.

"After what happened to Dawn…and leaving the way I did, with hardly any notice. The kids must feel I abandoned them. They would never be able to trust me again."

Mike placed his hand on Jeff's shoulder. "Didn't look that way to me when Jeremy approached you. He could have just walked away, but he didn't. Kids are a lot more forgiving than we are of ourselves, or even of them. Give them a chance, they might surprise you."

Jeff nodded thoughtfully. "I'm touched, Mike. Really I am."

"You're a wonderful pastor, Jeff. Sincere, passionate and energetic, the kids can sense that. They trust you."

"I appreciate your saying that."

"But?"

"But I need a little time to think about it. It's a huge step."

Mike smiled wide. "Wouldn't want you if you didn't."

Jeff held out his hand. "It was great to see you again. And to see all the progress you've made here. It's truly awesome."

"Thanks," Mike said. "To both of you. Now don't be strangers."

"You got it," Jeff said and led Willa around front to the car.

"I like him," Willa announced as they drove out of the rectory parking lot.

"He's a good guy."

"So are you."

He turned and looked at her, the anguish in his eyes breaking her heart.

"You didn't abandon them. You did what you had to do to deal with a tragedy. Don't be so hard on yourself."

He nodded, but looked away.

"How was church this morning? Any fallout from our trip?"

"Not much. Everyone is just relieved we're all safe." He gave her arm a squeeze. "You don't have to worry about the barbecue this evening. No one is going to dress you down and serve you up as the main course."

She grinned. "Thanks, that's good to know. Is your dad going to be there?" She hated the insecurity that entered her voice.

"He is. It'll be all right. I realize he's hard to swallow, especially lately."

"Lately?"

"I'm afraid he's concerned about our relationship."

"Oh?" Willa grinned. "We have a relationship?"

"I like to think so."

She looked at his profile as he drove down the freeway and admitted to herself that she would like to have a relationship with him. She wouldn't mind hearing his voice on her answering machine when she got home at night or exchanging stories about their day over dinner.

He turned and caught her staring at him.

What had he been saying? "Why would our, um, liking each other have your dad upset?"

"Well, it's not you personally—"

"Oh. I guess I'm from the wrong side of the tracks, eh?"

"No, you're from the right side, the side I came from, the side he's desperately afraid I'll go back to."

"But why? You've done great things here. You've made a real difference in the lives of many people. And yes, you're going to lose a few along the way, but look at all those you'll save. Has your father ever been down here? Has he seen what I've just seen?"

"No."

"Then perhaps he ought to make the trip."

Jeff smiled, though he didn't say anything.

"What?"

"I'm not sure I'm ready to go back."

"Of course you're ready." She looked at his face, which was troubled and serious. "Okay, I'll bite. Why not?"

"I'm not sure."

"Wasn't it you who preached my ear off with that

holier-than-thou attitude about changing the world through love and not hate, about going after the good with the good—yada, yada, yada.''

''I don't think I put it quite that way.''

''Whatever, you're the man of words here—I'm the woman of action. And right now I'm thinking you've been doing too much talking and not enough acting the last couple of years.''

''Willa—''

''No, hear me out. You have to do what's right for you, because in the end, you're the one who has to live with yourself. Just give it some thought, that's all I'm asking.''

He parked in front of a popular pie shop not far from the hotel. ''All right, I will. I have a feeling you aren't going to give me much choice.''

She smiled. ''Perhaps. Can I help it if you knock my socks off?''

His eyebrows lifted. ''I do?''

''Yep. You're quite an impressive fella.'' She leaned over to kiss his cheek, but he swiveled on her and she found her lips locked onto his. Wow, could that man kiss!

Chapter Twelve

After lunch Jeff and Willa entered the expansive lobby of the Montague Hotel and approached the front desk. "Has a Mrs. Evelyn Wilcox checked in yet?" Willa asked the stone-faced clerk.

"I'm sorry, we—"

Willa promptly presented her badge.

Immediately, he looked down at his screen and started typing. "No, ma'am."

"Thank you," she responded. They took a seat on a settee by the front doors and waited for Tracey and her mother to arrive. "I hope we can get them to change hotels."

"Do you really think it's necessary?"

"No." She sighed. "The smell of cigarette smoke could have drifted through my open window, but I prefer to be safe rather than sorry." She stole a quick glance around the spacious room. From their vantage point, she could easily see if Carlos was waiting. He wasn't.

Jeff took her hand. ''I'm really glad you're coming with me to the barbecue this evening. I want everyone to get a chance to know you better.''

''You mean your father?''

''You got me,'' he admitted. ''I think you're pretty special and I want him to think so, too.''

She smiled, glowing at his words. ''What makes you think he's going to like me any better this time than he did last time?''

''The circumstances of your meeting were a bit strained.''

''I'll give you that, but if he doesn't like strong women who carry guns, well then—'' she shrugged ''—I don't think there's much hope.''

''You're probably right. Female action heroes have never been his cup of tea.''

Willa laughed at the image. ''Is it that important to you?''

''You're important to me.''

She lost herself just gazing into the perfect blue of his eyes. How had she ever gotten so lucky? He cared about her. It seemed so unreal, and yet here he was looking at her as if she were the only woman on earth.

He grasped a tendril of her hair, letting the wild red curl wrap around his finger, then tucked it behind her ear. The simple gesture filled her with an overwhelming sense of happiness. She tried desperately to quash the goofy look she felt blossoming on her face, but couldn't. Instead she scooted closer to him. ''Are we going to have any time alone at this barbecue?''

''Maybe. What did you have in mind?''

She blushed at the image that popped into her head.

He cleared his throat before confessing, "I haven't dated much since my last relationship ended. I'm afraid I'm a bit rusty."

"No?"

"I haven't met anyone that has interested me enough to make the effort."

"Oh." His confession left her feeling immensely pleased.

"Nor have my feelings been strong enough to consider making a commitment."

A twinge of anxiety infringed on her pleasure. "Commitment?"

"Someone I've felt seriously enough about to get involved with. And if you make another monosyllabic sound, you'll be sorry."

"I—"

Instantly, his lips fell over hers in a possessive display that stole her breath. If ever there was a moment where she finally understood the meaning of the word *swoon,* this was it. The soft pressure of his lips over hers, the tender grasp of his hands on her shoulders, she was incapable of resisting.

Dazed, she was tremendously thankful she was already seated because, at that moment, her limbs were useless.

"Commitment," he said matter-of-factly.

"Yes, I see what you mean," she agreed and gently massaged her tingling lips. "You have me at an unfair advantage."

"Oh, yeah? How's that?"

"Your kisses keep knocking me senseless."

He gave her a triumphant look as Tracey and her

mother walked through the door. ''Jeff,'' Tracey squealed and flew into his arms.

''Hey, kiddo. How are you?'' The pure joy lighting Jeff's face made Willa smile. He was such a good man. A good man who wanted to be with her!

''Fine. Mom and I just had the best time in Oregon. We're thinking of moving there. We've decided we need a change.''

Jeff beamed. ''Glad to hear you're doing so well.''

Willa noticed the strain on Evelyn's face.

The woman gave her a wan smile. ''I didn't expect you would be here so soon.''

''We wanted to make sure you arrived all right.''

''Thank you. We're fine. Just tired. It was a long drive.''

''I can imagine. Mrs. Wilcox, if you wouldn't mind, I'd like to move you to a different hotel.''

Her shoulders sagged with weariness. ''Please, Miss Barrett. I'm sure the security at this hotel is adequate and no one but you know we're here. We're just going to grab a quick bite, then button down for the night.''

''I can see you're tired,'' Willa persisted. ''But your location could have been compromised. Someone could have been in my apartment when you were speaking on the answering machine last night.''

''But you don't know for sure?'' Evelyn asked.

''No,'' Willa admitted.

Evelyn hesitated. ''I know it would be the logical thing to do, but I've been driving for twelve hours straight and I can't move another step. If you want, you can collect us first thing in the morning and we'll go to the police station together to give our statement. I promise we won't leave our room."

"All right," Willa relented. "I understand." She did understand, but she didn't like it. She approached the front desk and informed the clerk that under no circumstances were they to reveal Mrs. Wilcox's room number to anyone, nor were they to verify that she was even staying in the hotel to anyone who called. The clerk nodded in agreement.

Before leaving, she left the same instructions for the manager. It was all she could do, and hopefully, it would be enough. They circled the hotel twice before departing, searching for anything out of the ordinary, but everything checked out fine.

"It's okay to be cautious," Jeff said.

"I know. But something doesn't feel right," Willa admitted.

"Do you want to go back and insist they move?"

"I should."

"But they did look tired, and the chance that someone was actually in your apartment at the exact moment they called is—"

"I know, slim to none." Willa let out a heavy sigh.

"There you go."

Perhaps she'd drop a line to Ben when they reached her apartment and fill him in. She smiled to herself. That would definitely be a change. "You know, you're kind of good for me," Willa announced, feeling better about leaving.

"Really? A kind of peanut butter to your jelly?"

"Hot fudge to my vanilla ice cream."

"You say the sweetest things."

"That's one I've never heard before," Willa said caustically.

Jeff laughed, and for the first time in she didn't know when, she was happy. "You know, Jeff, you've really helped Tracey. She loves you. All the kids from your church love you. You don't need to go back to L.A. to help children—you'll help kids wherever you are. And wherever you are, I'm sure there'll be kids like Tracey who need you."

He smiled and clasped her hand. "You're right. I can do just as much good here, as I can there. The real question is what kind of work do I want to be doing? Which is more fulfilling, personally?"

"That's a question only you can answer." They pulled into Willa's complex. "You coming up?"

"No, I have a lot of thinking to do."

"All right." She leaned over and gave him a soft kiss, and lowered her voice. "I'll see you in a couple of hours at the barbecue."

"I'm looking forward to it."

The foul smell assaulted Willa the moment she walked through the door. She opened the windows in the living room and bedroom, trying to get a cross draft to clear the odor that was growing in intensity. She checked under the sink for garbage that might have fallen behind the trash can, but didn't find any. If the smell got any worse, she'd have to call the manager. Perhaps an animal had crawled into the wall space and had become trapped within the walls.

She grimaced at the thought, lit a slew of candles, emptied a can of air freshener, and tried to put the distasteful odor out of her mind so she could concentrate on what she was going to wear to the church barbecue. She searched her closet, pulling out one dress after another, before finally admitting to herself how nervous she really was.

It was important that she make a good impression and win over Jeff's father. She didn't see any reason he wouldn't like her. She was a likable person, when she wanted to be. She finally selected a white frilly sundress that she'd bought for a wedding a few years back. She'd only worn it once, as the yards of creamy lace made her look soft and fragile—a look she usually hated, but one she'd relish today. She laid the dress out on the bed, then pulled open her fancy lingerie drawer for her silk camisole.

A huge rat, its teeth bared in a frozen endless snarl, lay atop a pillow of her best silk and satin lingerie. Willa stifled a scream, then stumbled against the bed, her heart hammering painfully inside her chest, her lungs struggling for breath. She gagged on the noxious smell that filled the room. Covering her nose and mouth, she ran into the kitchen. The poor beast hadn't been trapped in the wall, but carefully placed among her most intimate apparel.

Carlos!

She grabbed several plastic bags out of the cupboard and covered her face with a clean towel. Her stomach turned over several times in the twenty-second time span it took her to reach into the drawer and seize the rat's body with the plastic bag. Involuntarily, she retched, all the while praying she wouldn't throw up.

In her job, she'd seen worse things than this, but she'd never before had to clean them up.

Immediately, she stopped and dropped the bag. What was she doing? More than anything she just wanted to scoop the whole mess up and throw it in the trashbin out back. But what if Carlos had left something behind that could prove he'd been there?

What if he hadn't? Did she really want the cops back at the station examining all of her fancy underwear?

If she called the cops now, they'd keep her here at least an hour, probably two, as they sifted through everything in her apartment. And even if they did find something pointing to Carlos, which was doubtful, what good would that do? She didn't want him brought up on breaking and entering; she wanted him charged with kidnapping and attempted murder.

Then it hit her. *Carlos had been here.* He'd heard Evelyn's message. Unless Tracey's mother called after he'd left. There was always that possibility. She grasped on to the dim hope. Otherwise, the alternative was that he heard her call and knew exactly where they were.

She didn't have time to waste. She had to get to Tracey.

She picked up the bag with the dead animal, tied it tight, dumped the contents of the drawer into another bag, then threw the whole lot outside her front door. She ran to the phone and called the hotel. "Give me Evelyn Wilcox's room."

"Sorry, ma'am. She's left a message that she doesn't want to be disturbed."

Willa stifled a roar. ''This is Officer Barrett. I was there earlier—''

''Yes, of course, I remember—''

''Please put me through to her room. It is imperative that I speak with her, now.''

''I'm sorry ma'am, but I can't do that. I have no way of verifying who you are.''

Silently, Willa fumed.

''Let me ring her for you and I'll tell her you're on the line and will await her call.''

''Thank you,'' Willa muttered. ''I'll hang on until you've reached her.'' Please hurry, she thought, as she waited for the clerk to come back on the line.

''I'm sorry, ma'am, but there was no answer in Mrs. Wilcox's room.''

''Any chance they left?''

''I didn't see them.''

''Please ask security to send someone up to her room, I'll hold the line.''

He agreed, though reluctantly.

Ten excruciatingly long minutes later, the manager came back on.

''I'm sorry, but there isn't anyone in the room.''

''Does it look like they left unexpectedly?''

''Huh?''

''Were they forced to leave?''

''That I couldn't say,'' he replied, the concern evident in his voice. ''Do you think that's what happened? Should I call the police?''

''I *am* the police.''

''Oh, right. Yes, of course.''

She took a deep breath before speaking again. ''I'll

send someone over. In the meantime, please keep an eye out for Mrs. Wilcox and her daughter. Perhaps they just went out for a bite to eat."

"Yes, that could be, except…except they ordered room service an hour ago."

Willa muttered under her breath. "Great. Did they eat it?"

"I'm not sure. I didn't notice, I'm afraid. I can go back," he suggested.

"No, no. I'll send someone over. Don't let anyone in their room."

"Yes, ma'am."

"Thank you for your help." Willa hung up. Carlos had them. She knew it, felt it in the hair tingling on her nape and the sick dread twisting in her stomach. She called Ben and informed him of her suspicions.

"I'll send someone to check it out, but Willa, you stay out of it, understood?"

"But, Ben, this is my witness. I have a personal stake in this case."

"I mean it, Willa. Not this time. Chances are she got cold feet and split again."

"Yeah, right."

"You've lost your objectivity on this one, and besides that, you're off the case. Pete O'Donnelly's handling it now and he won't appreciate your interference."

Willa was sure he wouldn't. "Fine, but you won't object if I call him?"

"As long as you play by the rules, Willa. That's all I've ever asked of you."

"Absolutely. Oh, and Ben, I found a dead rat in my

underwear drawer. I don't think it got there on its own."

He swore. "All right, I'll send someone over there, too."

"I'll leave my door open."

"Willa?"

"Yeah."

"Keep out of trouble."

"You got it, boss."

Willa hung up the phone, not surprised in the least that the call had gotten her nowhere. But that wouldn't stop her. She just had one last thing to take care of, and she knew her next call wouldn't be as easy. Especially once she heard the excited tenor in Jeff's voice.

"I'm really sorry, Jeff, but I'm not going to be able to make it to the barbecue," Willa started.

"Why not? Has something happened?"

"I think Carlos has Tracey." She quickly explained about the rat and her conversation with the hotel manager.

Jeff took a deep breath. "Did you call Ben?"

"Yeah, he's got Pete on it."

"Then what are you hoping to do?"

"I want to stake out Jack's warehouse and do a little snooping around to see what I can find out."

"That doesn't sound like a very good idea. They came after you before, now you're going to go to them?"

"It's not like that," she insisted.

"Is Ben aware of your plan?"

"No, of course not."

"Willa, please. I don't think you should go near there alone. You need help, you need backup. Let Ben and Pete work this the way they want to. They—"

"I work alone, Jeff. I always have."

"Now's as good a time as any to change that. Call Ben, ask him to give you help."

"Jeff, Ben took me off the case. He doesn't want me anywhere near Carlos and I don't want him sending in someone who's going to blow it. Tracey is my responsibility."

"Since when?"

"Since I started to care about her."

"I care about you." His words were soft and quiet. "I don't want anything to happen to you."

"I can't let Jack and Carlos destroy another family."

"What about you? Willa, I'm worried.... At least let me come with you."

"I can take care of myself, I always have." She refused to budge. She wouldn't let him talk her out of this like she let him talk her out of leaving the hotel. She should have camped outside their door and stayed, all night if that's what it took. Why hadn't she followed her instincts? She'd let him distract her, let him deaden her instincts, and now a young girl might pay the price.

"How do you know about this warehouse?"

"I talked to some of the guys at the banquet last night. They told me about it."

"I didn't see you talking with anyone."

"You weren't watching my every move, Jeff. But

if you must know, it was when I went to the rest room.''

''Within five minutes you managed to find out where Jack was? Is that all you ever have on your mind? Jack and how to get to him, even when you're with me?''

''No, of course not,'' she said a little too forcefully. ''Maybe sometimes,'' she added. ''Look, I'm sorry that I can't be all that you want me to be, but I am who I am and I'm not changing. Not for you, not for the captain, not for anybody.''

''Not even for yourself? Can't you see that you're hurting people and isolating yourself because you're too focused on vengeance?''

''You know, I'm tired of surrounding myself with people who always have something to criticize me about. Why can't you appreciate who I am, everything that you like about me, along with those things you don't?''

He sighed. ''I do, believe me, I'm very aware of all your good qualities. It's your reckless desire for putting yourself in danger right now that has me concerned.''

''If you trusted me as a professional we wouldn't be having this discussion right now. All I really want to do is make sure Tracey and her mother are safe. I thought you, of all people, would understand that.''

''I do understand. I'm just as worried about Tracey as you are, but like you said, Ben's on it and I don't think it's very safe or rational to be taking on men like Jack and Carlos by yourself. I think you need to have a little faith and trust in your captain, and let him handle it.''

Faith and trust in Ben? And if he screwed up again? Tracey and her mother could end up just like her dad. ''I need to make sure Tracey's safe. Until then, I won't be able to rest. I don't have enough faith or trust in me for that. I'm sorry. Like I said, I really want to come to the barbecue with you. This is just something I have to do.''

''Let me come with you.''

''I can't. It's too dangerous.'' Not to mention she needed to be on her toes. She couldn't afford any distractions when dealing with a monster like Carlos.

''I just want you to be safe, Willa.''

''I will be, I promise. Perhaps you should have some faith in me.''

''Okay, fine. Call me when it's all over.''

The hollow thud of the receiver hanging up shot painfully through her heart, but she pushed it aside, hardened herself and focused on what she needed for her surveillance. She had work to do and she wouldn't let his wounded pride stop her from doing it.

Chapter Thirteen

Jeff sat at one of several long tables arranged throughout the church courtyard surrounded by smiling chatting people he'd come to know well over the last two years. With open arms they'd welcomed him into their families and homes. Even now, they talked excitedly about upcoming church events as they ate barbecue chicken, steak and potato salad. His heart should be full, but it wasn't.

Please, Lord, help me make the right decision. Help me find my path, he prayed silently. *And above all, keep a special eye out for Willa.* He was more worried about her than he cared to admit. As sure as he was that she could take care of herself, he also knew if anyone could find a way to land smack-dab in the middle of trouble, it was Willa. He just hoped she was wrong about Tracey.

"Hey, Jeff," Matt greeted and scooted onto the bench next to him. "How's it going?"

Jeff smiled at the teen, thankful for the diversion

from the road his thoughts were taking. "Just fine, and you? Any ill effects from our little adventure?"

"No way, man. That trip was totally awesome."

Jeff nodded. "You know, I thought so, too." The image of Willa smiling up at the giant Sequoias immediately came to mind.

"I was hoping Willa would be here tonight," Matt said, his gaze taking in the surrounding tables.

Jeff agreed. He'd been keeping an eye out for her, too, hoping she'd surprise him and tell him she'd changed her mind, and ask for his help.

"She is one cool lady," Matt continued. "The way she took off after those bad guys." His hand shot out in a fast-as-lightning gesture. "She didn't even flinch when they fired at us."

The excitement shining in the boy's eyes widened Jeff's smile into a knowing grin. "You kind of liked her, eh?"

Color filled Matt's cheeks. He dropped his head to examine his fingernails. "She's all right."

Jeff laughed and rustled Matt's hair. "You're pretty all right yourself."

Matt rose, looking a little embarrassed. "See ya," he called, then disappeared into a group of people lining up for cheesecake and chocolate cream pie.

"You have a special way with the kids," Jeff's father announced, as he sat in the space Matt had vacated.

"Thanks," Jeff mumbled under his breath. His father had never been generous with compliments unless he was using them as a means to achieve something.

Jeff could only imagine what his father had on his mind for him now.

"You're a great youth minister," he continued. "You are able to reach these kids, to keep them on the straight and narrow."

"I hope so," Jeff responded, and considered going after a piece of chocolate cream pie himself.

"Your mother would have been proud of you."

Jeff turned his attention from the dessert table back to his father. This was something he hadn't heard often. He tried to gauge the level of sincerity in his eyes, but his father wasn't looking at him. Instead, he was lost somewhere in the past, a flicker of pain outlining the sadness on his face.

Jeff's demeanor softened. As hard as his father had always been, Jeff knew he'd only had his best interest at heart. He had done the best he could, raising Jeff alone after his mother's death.

"Why haven't you ever remarried?" Jeff asked and he wondered why he hadn't thought to ask before.

"Never found anyone who could fill the emptiness she left in our lives." His father let out a heavy sigh. "Your mom was a real special lady."

His words, so close to the ones Jeff had spoken earlier with Matt, brought Willa's image to mind again.

"I hope you get lucky enough to find someone like her one day," his father continued. "Someone to help you serve God and His children."

Jeff nodded. He could finally see where this conversation was heading. *Willa.* Deciding to head him off at the pass, Jeff said, "I visited the Sun Valley

Church this morning, Dad.'' He paused for effect. ''I'd heard of the teen shelter they'd built and I wanted to see the progress they've made.''

His father looked up quickly, his eyebrows raised in surprise.

''It was quite impressive,'' Jeff continued. ''I couldn't believe how much they'd accomplished in the last two years.''

His father didn't respond.

Jeff took a deep breath and let the other shoe drop. ''They've asked me to come back.''

His father's lips thinned into a straight line of disapproval.

''I'd like you to come with me and see the wonderful advancements they've made. I think you'll be surprised and impressed.''

The blue in his father's eyes turned a cold, steely gray. ''I don't see how moving back to inner city Los Angeles to work with drug-abusing negligent hoodlums will further your career,'' he hissed through clenched teeth.

Startled by his malice, Jeff stared at his father in disbelief.

''You're on the right track here, Jeff. Do you realize how hard I had to work to get you this position? Now you're considering throwing it all away?'' His father stood, outrage hardening his features. ''I had hoped the lack of that woman's presence here tonight meant you'd seen the light and realized just where you belong, but I can see the damage has already been done.''

Embarrassment washed through Jeff as the family

seated closest to them rose from the table, sympathy filling their eyes as they looked at him. He tried to swallow his anger, as he had each and every time his father had bullied or used guilt to force him into a decision he hadn't wanted to make.

But not any longer.

Willa might be reckless and impulsive, but she was a straight shooter and she was strong enough to stand up for her principles and for herself. So could he.

Strength surged within him, deepening his voice. "Do you have so little faith in my judgment that you believe a few days with Willa Barrett can push me off the straight and narrow path of ambition you've so carefully perched me on? Have you ever thought, even for a second, that perhaps I get a great deal of fulfillment helping those poor, outcast, misled and sometimes drug-addicted *children?*"

Jeff rose, standing inches from his father and looked him straight in the eye. "Does the fact that they aren't comfortable and pampered make them any less worthy? What kind of man have you become?"

Reverend Edward MacPhearson sputtered with indignation.

"Pastor Mike is making wonderful strides helping those less fortunate than ourselves, and I intend to be a part of it. If you want to perform any type of role in my life, then you'll have to drive down to the city and see it all for yourself." Jeff started to walk away, then stopped. "You just might be surprised what you find, Dad."

He hurried to the parking lot, leaving his father staring after him, shocked into speechlessness. Jeff had to smile at that. He'd never seen his father at such a loss for words.

Willa was right. Some decisions just had to be made from the gut. She was right about one other thing, too; Tracey had to be found, and if the police couldn't find her, then it was up to them. And if she wouldn't let him join her, then he'd find her on his own.

Willa maneuvered her Jeep from east to west on K Street, her spirits falling as she was confronted with row after row of warehouses. Occasionally, she'd spot an iron-barred liquor store or some other small-front business, but nothing to help her. Without more accurate information, there was no way she'd be able to determine which of the look-alike warehouses belonged to Jack.

She swung the Jeep around and headed toward the strip. Someone at Jack's apartment building on Sunset Boulevard might know which warehouse was his. Otherwise, she'd have to call Pete and hope he'd do more than grunt at her. As she reached the strip, she drove slowly past the apartments, sensitive for anything unusual, but everything looked the same as it had before she'd left.

She parked two blocks down and trotted back up the street, searching for a familiar and friendly face among the foot traffic.

But none was found.

She slowed as she approached the front of the apartment building, reluctance growing within her. Should she go back in there? Could Carlos be waiting for her? She hesitated in front of the door leading into the building. Through the dirty glass, the staircase stood barren in the dark entryway. Tentatively, she glanced back at the street. The press of people milling about seemed to have thinned, leaving only a bystander here and there. Even though no one appeared interested in her, something didn't feel right.

Had Jack and Carlos expected her to return? Were they waiting for her even now as she stood alone on the sidewalk contemplating her next step? The unreasonable fear swelling inside her was both foreign and unexpected. She took a deep breath and placed her hand on the doorknob that was never locked.

Have a little faith, Willa. She did have faith—in herself and in the Beretta tucked in her purse. As she turned the knob, a blurred reflection of a man standing behind her appeared in the door's glass panel.

Pivoting, she demanded, "Hold it," as she drew her weapon from her purse.

Jeff's blue eyes widened in surprise and he took a step back from her, raising both hands. "Whoa, there."

"Jeff!"

"Didn't mean to startle you," he said calmly, though his eyes never left her gun.

"You scared the life out of me." Quickly she returned the gun to her purse.

"Sorry." He shrugged.

She stared at him, confusion wrinkling her brow. "What are you doing here?" He looked distant, his manner detached. Where was that charming smile that always managed to turn her into a pile of mush?

"Looking for Tracey. Don't worry, I won't interfere with your investigation."

His coldness unsettled her. "Oh." She took a deep breath, trying to calm her nerves. "All right then. Let's go have a look." She pushed open the door and climbed the steep staircase to the second floor. He was still mad at her for blowing off the barbecue. For blowing off him, more like it. As much as she didn't want him to come with her, she sure was glad he was there. Hushed voices belied a presence on the third floor. Her floor. Willa tried to clear her mind of Jeff and focus on her surroundings. But it wasn't easy.

Cautiously, they continued up. The voices, all female, were coming from Betty's apartment at the top of the stairs. She reached the landing, took a few steps to Betty's doorway, and peered in. Three young women she knew only as Sally, Mary and Bridget were surrounded by half-filled boxes. Willa blew out a sigh of relief. No sign of Jack or Carlos.

She gestured for Jeff to continue down the hall. "Mine's the one at the end," she whispered. Before she could say more, he'd slipped past her and hurried down the hall. Willa watched him walk away from her, and pushed back the sadness weighing heavily on her shoulders. Why hadn't she just included him? Why had she been so determined to go it alone? Because he's a civilian, she told herself. "Be careful," she whispered, but knew he was too far away to hear.

She stepped into Betty's open doorway. "Hey, Mary," she called to a woman wearing jean cutoffs and a psychedelic tube top. A bright-red scarf held back wild black curls as she pulled her head out of a kitchen cabinet and balanced a stack of dishes in her hand. Mary's dominant personality had always made her the leader, especially with the younger women who were scared and unsure of themselves.

A look of disbelief crossed the woman's face as she stared at Willa. ''Hey, girl, aren't you a surprise? I almost didn't recognize you without your wig.'' She paused, her eyes narrowing. ''We all thought you bit the dust.''

''Yeah, big time,'' Sally, who was dressed in a yellow sundress cut way too short, added while carefully placing wineglasses in a sectioned box. Wherever Mary was, Sally wouldn't be far behind. The third girl, Bridget, took a box and disappeared into a back room.

''Really,'' Willa responded casually. ''What gave you that idea?''

''Betty told us what Carlos did to you, the nasty things he'd said,'' Sally replied, her thick black brows rising with the excitement of telling a secret.

'''Real ugly,' is what Betty said. I can't believe you'd show your face around here again after that.'' Mary crossed the living room and parted the curtains, looking down into the alley behind the building.

''Besides, I saw you on the news. Is it true you're a cop?''

Willa nodded.

''Then get out. We don't want anything to do with you.''

''I'm not here to cause any of you trouble. I never was. It's Jack I want. And Carlos.''

''You're lucky Carlos is not here now. That man's major sick, and he's got it in for you.''

Tell me about it, Willa thought. "Where's Betty?"

"You ain't heard?" Mary asked, turning from the window.

"No, what?" Dread pinched the base of Willa's spine.

"Betty's dead. Someone carved her up real bad."

Willa gasped, not knowing what upset her more—what Mary had said, or the matter-of-fact tone she'd used to say it. Although she didn't know why she was so surprised; this was an ugly business and ugly things happened every day. Willa swallowed the sour taste in her mouth. "Someone or *Carlos?*"

They wouldn't meet her gaze. It was all the answer she needed. Mary crossed the room and reached behind Willa to close the door. "Now don't be talking 'round here like that or we'll all be getting what Betty got," Mary said softly. "She always did talk too much and you know it."

"About what?"

"'Bout nothing."

Carlos had done an excellent job silencing these women and probably all the others in the building, too. Poor Betty had been the example he'd used to make sure they'd all keep quiet. Guess they were all useful to him after all—useful and expendable.

Willa opened the door and glanced down the hallway. No sign of Jeff. She left the door opened a crack, then lifted a picture from the table next to her. In it, a much younger Betty stood with an older couple who smiled wide for the camera. What had happened to her? How had she gotten so messed up?

Bridget came back into the room and placed her full

box by the door. She taped the ends shut, then wrote Bedroom on the top with a permanent black marker.

"Who were these people?" Willa asked, waving the picture at them. "Her parents? Does anyone know who they are or how to reach them? Are they even still alive?" She stared at their blank faces. "Do any of you care? Or are all of you so wrapped up in your own miserable and shallow existences that you've forgotten Betty was a person with a family and prayers and dreams? These were her things—this was her life!"

She kicked the box as unshed tears burned in her eyes. "Carlos and Jack stole that from her, and they're stealing it from you, too. Minute by minute, day by day, and you're letting them."

"And what about you, Blondie?" Mary demanded. "What is it that keeps you coming back? The thrill? The adrenaline rush? Or is there something else you thrive on?"

Mary's question hit closer to home than Willa cared to admit. What *was* she doing there? Why hadn't she gone with Jeff to the barbecue? Instead she'd caused a rift between them, and who knew if they'd be able to bridge it? Who knew if she'd ever be able to enjoy a safe and normal life? She caught a glimpse of herself in the mirror and was surprised by what she saw. Eyes sharp with coldness took in the hard lines of determination that were becoming permanently etched into her face.

What was the point of her being there? These women didn't care about themselves any more than they cared about Betty's death. Anger rose in her, tightening her chest. ‘‘I’ve heard Jack and Carlos moved operations to a warehouse on K Street. I believe they’ve taken a thirteen-year-old girl with them, and I mean to get her back. Is anyone interested in helping me save her life, and perhaps reclaiming one for yourselves?’’

‘‘You’re crazy,’’ Mary insisted. ‘‘I’m not hearing anymore of this.’’ She stalked past her out the door with Sally tagging close behind her.

‘‘Me, either,’’ Sally snapped over her shoulder.

‘‘What about you, Bridget?’’ Willa asked the fresh-faced girl who couldn’t have been more than eighteen. ‘‘Are you going to hightail it out of here, too? Or are you going to do something to make sure you don’t end up like Betty?’’

‘‘What can *I* do?’’ the girl insisted. ‘‘I don’t know anyone here. There isn’t anything I even know how to do.’’

‘‘There’s a lot you can do. For starters, you can tell me about Jack’s warehouse. Have you ever been there?’’

She nodded.

‘‘Well?’’ Willa stepped closer; the girl backed away. She knew she was intimidating her, could see it in the uncertainty playing across her face. But she didn’t care. She wasn’t going to lose anyone else to Jack. ‘‘Please,’’ she pleaded. ‘‘Help me.’’

‘‘He has parties there,’’ Bridget whispered. ‘‘Special parties.’’

Willa’s mouth went dry. She could only imagine what *special* meant.

‘‘Which warehouse is it?’’

"I don't know," the girl answered. "I've only been there a couple of times, and I didn't pay that much attention."

Willa didn't suppose she had. "Is there anything you can tell me that will help me find this place? Anything at all?"

Tears swam in her eyes. "Do you think Betty hurt awfully bad?"

Willa bit her lip. Yeah, she supposed she had. The girl dropped her face into her hands and began to sob. Relenting, Willa put her arm around her shoulders and rubbed her back, trying to offer whatever comfort she could. "You know what?" she asked, softening her tone. "I have a friend close by. He can give you a place to stay, food to eat and someone to talk to. Someone you can trust until you get back on your feet."

Bridget looked up, hope and doubt commingling on her face.

"He'll ask nothing from you in return, I swear. He can help you, and he can teach you how to take care of yourself. Think you can handle that?"

Willa heard a movement in the hall and peeked out to find Jeff standing there. She grabbed his arm and pulled him into the room.

Bridget stiffened.

"He's okay, he's a friend," Willa said quickly. "So, what do you say?"

Bridget gave her a shaky smile. "After this place, I think I can handle just about anything."

"Good."

Willa turned to Jeff. ''Think Pastor Mike can handle one more?''

''Absolutely,'' he said, a genuine smile lighting his face as he introduced himself to Bridget. They led her out of the apartment and down the stairs to Willa's Jeep.

They drove the few blocks to Sun Valley Church in silence. Willa could tell Bridget was nervous, but Pastor Mike put her immediately at ease. They got her settled in the little house in back. The welcome the other girls showed Bridget pleased Willa and she promised her she'd return the next day to check on her.

Willa stopped outside the front door and watched Jeff and Mike in the yard, conversing and shaking hands before Mike pulled Jeff into a big bear hug. Willa couldn't help the smile spreading across her face. Jeff had made his decision.

She took a moment to privately celebrate his happiness then composed herself. If he'd wanted her to share this moment, he would have included her. He was all business now. She'd let him down. He was there for Tracey, not for her.

She pulled her cell phone out of her purse, punched in Pete's number, and hoped for the best.

''Sure, I'll tell you where the warehouse is,'' Pete responded after she'd explained why she'd called.

''You will?'' Willa asked, surprised.

''Absolutely. I'll be happy to give you enough rope to hang yourself.''

Willa sighed heavily. She didn't need this. Not now.

''You're a rotten cop, Willa. You're smart enough

and gutsy enough, but all you think about is what you want and that makes you dangerous.''

His words cut her to the core. ''I hardly think you're being fair—''

''You don't have what it takes, kid. And luckily, Ben is finally starting to do something about it.''

She'd always given the department everything she had. Why couldn't they appreciate that? Why didn't they care? ''I've always done the best job I could. My track record has been good,'' she said softly. ''Very good. Even you have to admit that, Pete.''

''What good is solving a case if a cop winds up dead?''

''What good is letting a cop killer go free?'' Bitterness rang heavy in her voice.

''We did everything we could to bring Jack to justice for what he did to your dad. We just didn't have enough proof. Witnesses were killed. You have to let it go and stop blaming us.''

''He was my dad. I can't let it go. You were there. Why can't you understand what this means to me?''

''Your dad was a great cop and my friend. And it's because he was my friend that I'm telling you you're dangerous. Please give up and get help. Face it, Willa, you will never be the cop your dad was.''

A large lump formed in her throat. ''My dad did whatever it took to get the job done,'' she said, groping to control the tears burning her eyes.

''Your dad did whatever he could for a fellow officer. That always came first, don't kid yourself. The case came second. Always. I hate to break it to you, kiddo, but you're nothing like your dad. You couldn't care less about your fellow officers. You're more like the guys we try to put away—relentless and self-delusional. It's time you grow up and stop playing cops and robbers, before someone gets hurt.''

Tears of shame flooded her eyes and cheeks. How could he think she didn't care? Of course, she cared. That was her problem. She cared too much. Why couldn't he see that?

''Do yourself a favor, Willa, and go home.''

''I'm sorry, Pete. But I can't do that.''

Chapter Fourteen

Willa wasn't certain if Pete's information had been worth it. He'd put her through the emotional wringer and now she just wanted to curl up in bed with a pint of pistachio ice cream. She turned down K Street and drove slowly, searching for the address Pete had given her. "Right over there," Jeff said, pointing to a nondescript building. Willa parked the Jeep along the curb opposite the warehouse. "Looks quiet," Jeff added.

Twilight had fallen, and except for a random unbroken streetlight, everything lay in shadows. Willa reached across Jeff and opened the glove box, more aware of his close proximity than was comfortable. He still hadn't said more to her than was absolutely necessary, and his obvious disappointment in her was making it more and more difficult for her to concentrate.

If only he would smile at her, or wink, or look at her with the same tender expression he had used this afternoon in the hotel lobby, the stretch of tension across her shoulders would dissipate. She knew he was angry with her, so why not yell? Scream? Get it out in the open—anything would be better than the cold distance he was showing her now. Why was she surprised he'd given up on her? She'd pushed him away. What did she expect? Like Pete, he thought she didn't care.

Grabbing her flashlight, she was careful not to touch him as she pulled it free of the compartment. Something dropped from the glove box and landed in his lap.

He held it up to the fading light. "My whistle."

"I'm sorry," Willa said softly. "I guess I forgot to return it to you when we got back from the mountains." She hadn't forgotten, not really. She just wanted something of his to hold on to.

"No need," he replied, and swiveled in his seat to face her. "I want you to keep it." Once again, he placed the whistle's long cord around her neck. "If you get lost—"

"Hug a tree?" She smiled ruefully, tears tightening her throat. He was the best thing that had ever happened to her and she'd blown it. She hadn't trusted him to help her.

"Or if you need me, blow the whistle and I'll find you."

"Thank you," she whispered, a sad smile lifting the corners of her mouth. "Jeff, I'm very happy for you, for your decision to go back to Sun Valley. I know it was the right one."

"Me, too."

"I'm sorry about tonight. I know how much you

wanted me to be with you.'' A leaden silence sat between them as Willa played with the whistle around her neck. His cologne tickled her nose and the desire to snuggle into his arms and lay her head against his chest was overwhelming. ''I've never been very good at making room in my life for other people, for what they want and need...but I'm willing to try with you. I want you to know that I do care about you.''

''I heard what you said to those women back there at the apartment building,'' Jeff said quietly.

''Yeah?'' Willa struggled to grasp what he was referring to. She'd just opened her heart, handing it to him on a silver platter, and he ignored it.

''About giving your life to Jack.''

''Oh?'' He didn't want her, after all. They were too different. It had just taken him a while to see it.

''You were right about what you said to them.''

An ache she'd never felt before squeezed the inside of her chest and lodged a large lump in the bottom of her throat. ''I was angry.''

''You've also given Jack a big chunk of *your* life.''

''I hardly think it's the same thing,'' she said, and tried to focus on keeping the welling tears at bay.

''Isn't it? God has given you many great gifts. It's true you've had adversity—you were dealt a bad hand with your father's death—but so have a lot of other people. Everyone has had bad days and has had bad things happen to them. The key is to deal with it, take whatever good out of it you can, and let the rest go. Don't let the anger consume you.''

''I understand what you're saying. But it's not that easy. I can't forget. No matter how hard I try.''

He placed his hands over his face and rubbed his eyes. ''I can't remember.''

''What's that?''

''My mother. I lost her when I was four. I can't recall her face or her voice, not even her smell. It breaks my heart.''

Stunned, Willa groped for a response. ''I'm sorry, I didn't know.''

''My point is that you don't have to forget. Instead of dwelling on the pain and anger, focus on the happiness and love your father brought into your life. Many people out there care for you, but one by one you've turned your back on them. The most precious gifts that God has given to you are love and friendship—don't you think it's about time you accepted them?''

A solitary tear coursed down her cheek. ''You just don't understand.''

''I know that God's love heals. Why can't you accept His gifts? And accept Him?''

They sat in silence while Willa tried to absorb his words. She hadn't known about his mother. If she had… She felt like such a fool, going on and on about her pain, her loss. He must think she was the most self-absorbed woman he'd ever met.

''Listen, I'm going to take a walk,'' Jeff announced.

''You're what?''

''Just down the street aways. And if I can, I'd like to check out the back of the warehouse.''

''Then I'm going with you.''

''No, you need to stay here and watch for Tracey.''

''I can't let you go out there alone,'' she said softly.

"Why not?"

"Something could happen to you. You need me to watch your back."

"I thought I was watching yours."

"Exactly," she said, grasping for something to say, some way to keep him with her. "I need you to stay here and watch mine."

He leaned across the seat and kissed her tenderly on the cheek, his lips leaving a warm tingly impression. She touched her cheek, as he opened the door.

"Please don't go," she whispered.

"I'll only be gone a second." He got out and closed the door. As she watched him cross the street, she brought the whistle to her lips and softly blew, filling the Jeep with the high-pitched sound. But he didn't turn. Instead, he crossed the street and disappeared into the darkness.

Please watch over him, Lord. Bring him back to me, safe. Willa's eyes widened in surprise. She'd just prayed! She couldn't remember ever having prayed before. But she had once, and the memories from the night her father had been shot came rushing back to her. She'd prayed for God to bring him back, to make the hurt go away. But her dad hadn't come back and the horror of the aftermath still hadn't gone away; she was living it, hour by hour, day by day.

With sudden clarity, she realized what Jeff had been trying to tell her. She had to let Jack go. If she didn't, he'd always have a hold on her. She'd have Jack and Carlos on her mind, day after day, for the rest of her life. They'd consume her.

She had been wasting her life, just like Mary and

Sally, because she couldn't move on, and what was worse, she'd been resentful and angry with Ben and everyone else who had moved on. Not anymore. She didn't like the woman she'd become any more than she liked the reflection she'd seen of herself in Betty's mirror.

She wanted to be happy and she wanted to love, and Lord, she wanted Jeff. She only hoped it wasn't too late and that she hadn't driven him too far away. One thing was sure: she wasn't going to leave him alone out there for another second.

She slipped on her holster, strapped in her gun and grabbed the flashlight. Just as she was about to open the door, a car turned onto K Street a quarter-mile down, heading straight toward her. Willa swore and slouched low in the seat as the car slowed and pulled into the warehouse across from her.

Jack's warehouse.

She peeked out the window as the large roll-up door started to close. A head turned in the back seat of the black sedan.

Tracey!

Quickly, she dug her cell phone out of her pocket and punched in Ben's number. "Ben, it's Willa," she said after he answered. "I'm sitting outside Jack's warehouse on K Street and I just saw a car pull in."

Ben sighed heavily. "Willa, what are you doing there? Why don't you ever listen to—"

"Ben, Tracey was in the back of that car."

"No matter how many times I tell you to stay away from Jack—"

"Ben!" Willa yelled in exasperation. "I'm calling

for backup. I need you to get down here pronto and watch my back.'' Ben was silent for a moment Willa was sure would never end.

''I'm on my way, sweetheart.''

Tears sprang to Willa's eyes at the endearment she hadn't heard in more years than she cared to remember. ''Thanks, Ben.''

She disconnected the line and prayed again. ''Come on, Jeff. Come back. Please,'' she muttered. *Lord, where could he be?* She scanned the dark recesses for so long her eyes burned. What if something had happened to him? She couldn't take it. He'd come to mean so much to her. She loved him. The realization hit her hard. *She loved him!*

Several minutes later Ben pulled up behind her car. She bolted from the Jeep, running to his side. ''Jeff went for a walk right before I called you and he still hasn't returned. Ben, I'm scared. What if something's happened to him?''

''Don't worry. We'll find him.''

She nodded as they crossed the road, and prayed he was right.

''There's most likely a security system,'' he said under his breath as they approached the warehouse.

''Maybe we should circle round back?'' That was the last place she saw Jeff go. Perhaps he was back there, lying unconscious in an alley, a broken bottle in shards around his head. Willa quashed the thought and focused on the building as she followed Ben down the alley. Her fear for Jeff was wreaking havoc with her ability to concentrate. She had to focus or she wouldn't be able to do her job and she could get them all killed.

A strange sort of relief mixed with anxiety over where he could be overcame her as they neared the back alley and found no sign of him.

"Looks like your young man found a way in," Ben said, pointing to an unlatched back window directly above a large blue Dumpster.

Willa gasped. "He went in alone? What was he thinking?"

Ben gave her a look of exasperation. "You of all people should know the answer to that."

"It's different with me," she mumbled.

"The only difference is that *you* care about him."

She smiled. "You must be right because the thought that anything bad has happened to him is totally messing me up."

He patted her on the shoulder. "Well, get yourself together, Barrett, so we can pull your young man's butt out of the fire."

"You got it. I'm fine. Really."

"Good, 'cause I'm depending on you."

Pride swelled in her chest. "I won't let you down."

He winked, then climbed to the top of the Dumpster and disappeared through the window. Willa followed close behind him, slowly letting herself drop into the dark warehouse. She switched on her flashlight and shone it around the room. They were in a storage area surrounded by large crates and boxes.

Ben said, "Jack must be getting into the import export business."

''Yeah, I can only imagine what his product must be,'' Willa said dryly.

''Let's not even go there,'' Ben cautioned. ''We need to concentrate on finding the girl and your friend.''

''You know,'' she whispered, as they made their way through the maze of boxes, ''I didn't see Tracey's mother in the car.''

A grim look fell over Ben's face, but he didn't say a word as they approached the door at the edge of the room. Ben cracked it open, nodded, then stepped into the lighted hallway. Adrenaline surged through Willa at the heightened risk of exposure. The first door they opened led to an empty gaming parlor draped in rich shades of velvet. She let out a deep breath. ''All clear.''

The next room revealed a salon, and farther down the hall, several bedrooms. ''Where are they?'' she whispered, growing impatient.

Ben's shoulders lifted in a shrug. With the next door they opened, they found Tracey.

Willa stared in shocked disbelief. Tracey's lithe arms bound at the wrists were extended above her head and tied to the wall. Her chin rested against her chest while her head drooped to one side. ''Oh, Tracey!'' Willa rushed to the girl, quickly untied her, and looked to Ben for help as Tracey slumped into her arms. ''Tracey, it's Willa.'' She patted the girl's cheeks, trying to rouse her. Ben grabbed her wrists, rubbing the chafed skin together, then felt for a pulse.

''Willa?'' the girl moaned.

''Yes, sweetie, I'm here.''

''Willa—'' Tears filled her eyes, spilling onto her cheeks. ''Willa, he killed my mom.'' She wrapped her arms around Willa's neck and cried, her small body wracking with sobs.

''We've got to get her out of here,'' Ben said.

Willa nodded. ''Tracey, did they hurt you? Can you walk?''

''They didn't touch me. They called me merchandise.''

Willa's shoulders sagged with relief. ''Come on, sweetie. Let's get going.''

Tracey nodded, a fresh stream of tears wetting her face. ''That man, Carlos, showed up in our room. He pointed a gun at me and my mom and made us go with him. When we got to the car, he hit her on the head with his gun. Blood was everywhere.''

The horror in her eyes broke Willa's heart. ''Shh, we'll talk about it later after we get you safe.'' She wrapped her arm around Tracey's shoulders offering comfort and guiding the girl back to the storage room. They threaded their way through the boxes back toward the window.

''He shoved her into the trunk of the car,'' Tracey continued, not able to let it go.

Willa understood her need to talk it out. ''The black one I saw you arrive in?''

Tracey nodded. ''You saw me arrive?''

''Yep, I was right out front in my Jeep, hoping I'd find you.''

Tracey looked reassured, but only for a second before her face fell again. Willa knew there was a chance Mrs. Wilcox was still alive, she just wasn't sure she'd be able to get to her, and she didn't want to raise the girl's hopes in case she was wrong.

"Okay, Tracey, up you go," Ben said and boosted her up to the window, but before she could push herself through, the warehouse flooded with light.

As Jeff opened his eyes, a blinding pain shot around the side of his head and ruptured through his right temple. The light pierced his eyes. The last thing he remembered was dropping through the window and onto the warehouse floor, before pain exploded through his head. It was no coincidence that that window had been left open. Someone had been waiting for him.

They had set a trap for Willa and he'd walked right into it. Splinters pushed into his shoulders. They'd bound his hands and shoved him into a crate. Painfully, he worked his way onto his knees so he could see over the top edge of the box.

Carlos stood not ten feet away leaning against a crate, his back to Jeff.

"I was hoping you'd show up," Carlos said to someone in the doorway. Jeff slumped back into the box. The quick movement brought searing pain pulsating through his head. He grimaced, fighting back a wave of nausea, applied pressure to his temple and tried not to utter a sound.

"I figured once we nailed your boyfriend, you wouldn't be too far behind."

"Where's Jeff?" Willa demanded.

Carlos laughed. "Don't worry, you'll be joining him real soon."

Willa! Jeff gasped. He had to get out of this box! And he had to do so without making any quick or jarring movements. Gingerly, he peeked over the edge, trying to locate something to cut the rope around his wrists. About twenty feet in front of him, Carlos stood pointing a gun at Willa's chest.

Fury swelled through him. Be careful, Willa, he begged her silently. Movement in the corner of his eye caught his attention. Tracey sat perched in the window, her big, fear-ridden eyes locked onto his. *Lord, let her make it, let them all make it.*

"Go, Tracey," Willa yelled, and stepped forward to push the girl out the window, but Ben beat her to it giving the girl a hearty shove. Jeff threw himself out of the box, landing on the concrete floor with a bone-jarring thud. A shot rang out. Willa screamed.

Oh, no! Willa!

Willa's vision shifted, displaying a distorted image of Ben, a grimace of pain crossing his face as he fell in slow motion to the floor. "Ben," she screamed. Her voice sounding muffled, echoed through her mind. She fell to the side of the man that meant more to her than she had ever realized. Blood soaked through the front of his shirt. Tears clouded her eyes. She applied pressure to the deep wound in his chest and screamed as loud as she could. "Run, Tracey, run."

"Don't worry, Blondie. We'll find her, just like we found the reverend when he ran."

Mind-numbing terror overcame her at his words. Jeff!

"Thanks to the L.A. news, we've learned quite a bit about you, Detective Willa Barrett."

Don't let him be dead, God. Willa prayed. *Get us out of this and I'll never be reckless again. Please, Lord. Don't let him be dead. I love him.*

"Like for instance, you're the daughter of the famous Wilkes Barrett, the cop we took out at Bobbi's Liquor store."

Willa's breath caught at the mention of her father's name.

"He was getting too close for our comfort, so he was removed. Permanently," Carlos bragged. "I'd only planned on paralyzing him to serve as a warning to others, but he got lucky and died."

Willa shuddered at the cold deliberation in which he spoke. Pain from a wound that refused to heal ached anew.

"We know you joined the force to avenge his death, Blondie."

Warm blood seeped through her fingers. "Hang in there, Ben. Hang in there," she whispered. But even as she said the words she feared none of them were going to make it out of there alive.

"There's one more thing we learned about you, Willa," Jack added as he joined them. "We learned you're a rogue cop. Your colleagues on the force don't care for you much. Which is too bad. It seems you like to work alone and you frequently refuse to call for help. Instead you rush headlong into foolish and dangerous situations. A lot like the one you find yourself in now."

Willa's eyes widened with surprise.

"We counted on that little tidbit tonight and you didn't let us down. We knew you'd come after the girl. And now we've got you, too. It seems as if all our problems have worked themselves out." Jack turned toward the door. "I can count on you to clean up here, Carlos? I've got a game in twenty minutes."

"Sure thing, boss."

Willa watched as Jack left the room. None of her previous hatred or animosity reared its ugly head. He didn't matter to her now; all that mattered was that the three people she cared about most make it out of this mess alive. *Lord, where is Jeff!*

Still, Jack's words gnawed at her. They had counted on her working alone. They had set this trap for her, and because of her, Jeff and Ben walked right into it.

"I'm sorry, Ben," she cried. "I'm so sorry." She dropped her head onto his shoulder.

"It's okay, sweetheart," Ben said softly. "He was wrong."

"He was?"

"You did call for backup. You called me." His reassuring smile faltered on his lips and his eyes drifted closed as he lost consciousness.

"Ben?" She shook his shoulder as her throat tightened with tears.

"All right, Blondie," Carlos sneered. "Throw me your weapon and move away from the old man."

Willa glared up at him and pulled her gun out of its holster. She should just shoot him. They weren't going to make it out of there anyway. Perhaps this way she'd take him out, too.

"Don't even think about it," he warned.

A movement behind Carlos caught her attention. Tufts of sun-washed hair stuck out from behind a crate. *Jeff?* She slid the gun across the floor, making sure it flew past Carlos. She only hoped it went far enough.

"That wasn't very nice, Blondie," Carlos said. "I'll remember that when I have *you* handcuffed to the wall."

Willa shivered at the image. Yep, she should have shot him. Carlos went for her gun. She started to rise. A shot echoed through the room. She dropped back to her knees covering Ben, fear hammering her chest.

The door at the front of the room burst open as Pete rushed in, a swat team right on his tail.

Willa's head dropped to Ben's shoulders and she burst into tears. "You called backup, didn't you, Ben?" He didn't respond. "They're here, Ben. You're going to be all right. They've come to get us. They didn't let you down."

Pete dropped to their side. "Is he okay?"

"I don't know," Willa admitted. And for the first time in her life, she couldn't think, couldn't move. She just looked around her, searching the room. Where was Jeff?

Pete pulled out his radio. "Bring the medics in here, stat!"

"Are you okay?" he asked gently.

She nodded. But she wasn't.

"We need paramedics over here," someone yelled from behind a cluster of crates.

"Jeff?" A surge of fear-driven adrenaline pumped through her. She jumped to her feet and ran around the crates. Carlos, not Jeff, lay motionless on the floor. She didn't spare him a second glance as she rounded the corner. She found Jeff lying against a crate, still holding her gun, blood coursing down the side of his temple.

Carefully, one of the officers removed the gun from his hand. Willa dropped to his side. "Jeff, are you all right?" He didn't look all right. His eyes held an unusual blank stare.

"I killed him," he whispered. "I killed a man."

Willa nodded. "You did what you had to do. Thanks to you, we're all going to be okay." She hoped.

"I let the anger overcome me and I took his life."

Willa watched as the paramedics lifted Jeff onto the gurney. "I'll meet you at the hospital as soon as I find Tracey," she said.

"I shot someone," he mumbled. Willa felt sick. She'd done this to him. She knew he could never fit into her world, and yet she wouldn't let him go. Fresh tears slid down her cheeks as she watched them wheel him out of the door.

She returned to Pete who was opening crates and thoroughly searching the warehouse.

"They've already taken Ben."

She nodded. He'd be okay. He had to be. "Did you find a young girl outside?"

"Tracey Wilcox?"

Willa nodded, grimly. "Yeah."

Pete shook his head.

"Can I have a couple of your men to help me search for her? Ben pushed her out that window," she gestured toward the window above them, "right before Carlos shot him."

Pete nodded. "I'll help you."

On their way out the door, he called a few more of his men.

"Also, Tracey said Carlos hit her mother with his gun and placed her in the trunk of his car. There's a chance she could still be alive."

Pete swore, then got back on his radio. "Have two more paramedics meet me in the garage." He hurried toward the front of the building.

Willa went on alone. She was moving in a foggy daze she couldn't seem to shake. She had to find Tracey. She wiped Ben's blood off her hands onto her jeans, and tried desperately to remove the last image she had of Jeff from her mind as she ran around the back of the building, searching for Tracey.

"Come on, Tracey. Where are you?" Defeat overcame her. She was gone. She was just gone. She circled back around to the front of the building, and thought of her whistle. Would she come for the whistle? Ridiculous.

But out of hope and options, she walked toward her Jeep and her cell phone. She had to call Jeff's father. She had to tell him Jeff was in the hospital, and why. Nausea churned in her stomach. The man wasn't going to take this well. She'd managed to do just what he'd feared she would. She had destroyed his only son.

She tried to open the door, but it was locked. She took out her keys, unlocked the door and found Tracey crouched on the floor, her face wet with tears.

"Tracey!"

''I'm sorry,'' she cried. ''I heard the shots and I ran and ran. I was so afraid they'd find me.''

''Shh. It's okay. You're going to be all right. Come on, the police are here and the ambulances. You need to go to the hospital.''

Tracey nodded. ''Are you sure it's okay to come out?''

Willa forced herself to smile. ''Yes, I'm sure.'' She held out her hand and the girl took it. As they walked toward the ambulance, the paramedics were wheeling out another gurney.

Before Willa could shield Tracey's eyes, she screamed, ''Mommy!'' And ran to the gurney. ''Is she all right?''

''We don't know yet, honey,'' Pete answered. ''She's lost a lot of blood, but the paramedics are taking good care of her. Here, hop in. You can ride with her to the hospital.''

Willa watched as Tracey climbed into the back of the ambulance with her mother and grabbed hold of her hand.

''You, too, Willa,'' Pete announced.

''But I have to call Jeff's father,'' she said, looking back toward her Jeep.

''I'll do that. You need to get checked out.''

''I'm fine.''

''You don't look fine, and I believe I'm in charge here.''

Willa looked up at him and smiled before tears overcame her. She nodded, unable to speak. He turned to go, but she touched his arm, stopping him. ''Pete?''

"Yes?"

"Thank you for coming."

He looked at her in surprise. "That's my job, Willa."

Chapter Fifteen

Reluctantly, Willa treaded alone down the hospital's corridor, exhaustion burning her eyes as she followed the glossy white aggregate tiles. She was beat, emotionally spent and at a total loss of what she could say to Jeff to help him.

Her stomach twisted with guilt as she approached his room. His doctor had assured her he was fine, suffering only a mild concussion. But it wasn't his physical state she was worried about.

Tentatively, she cracked open his door. He lay in bed sleeping, his father keeping vigil by his side. Willa let the door glide silently shut. ''Coward,'' she muttered to herself. She continued down the corridor toward Ben's room, her heart growing heavier with each step. She stood before the closed door, afraid of what she'd find upon opening it.

Would Margo ever be able to forgive her for dragging Ben into this mess? Captains don't usually find themselves in the line of fire.

"You gonna stand out there all day?"

Willa closed her eyes, took a deep breath, then turned to face Pete. "Is he okay?"

"Open the door and see for yourself."

She held Pete's gaze, searching for the truth in his crystal clear eyes, but she couldn't find it. She opened the door. Before she could take stock of the situation, Margo had her in her arms squeezing the life out of her.

"I'm so sorry," Willa said, on a shaky breath.

"Don't be silly. It's not your fault. I'm just glad you weren't hurt, too. And that everything worked out."

Had everything worked out? Willa stole a glance at the hospital bed. Ben was lying there, a big bandage covering his chest, an even larger smile crossing his face.

"Ben!" Willa ran to his side, and enveloped him in a big hug, careful of his wound but overjoyed to see his smile once again directed at her. "Are you going to be okay?"

"Of course. It will take a lot more than one measly bullet to bring me down."

Willa laughed. "Yep. You're too cranky for that."

"You'd better believe it. How's that young man of yours?"

Instantly, she sobered, her good mood quashed under the weight falling across her shoulders. "A slight concussion is all. They're keeping him overnight for observation."

"Good. Glad to hear it. And the girl's mother?"

"Looks like she's going to make it," Pete answered.

Willa let out a sigh of relief. They were all okay, except for Jack and Carlos. They finally had enough evidence on Jack to put him behind bars for many years, and Carlos… Well, Carlos wouldn't be hurting anyone anymore.

"You look beat, sweetie," Margo stated. "Why don't you call it a night?"

Willa smiled gratefully. "Thanks. I think I will." She longed for sleep—quiet, blissful, forgetful sleep.

Jeff cracked open a bleary eye, saw his father's head bowed in prayer and quickly closed it again. Was he dead? No, he hurt too bad to be dead. This time he opened both eyes. "Dad?" The word came out a croak. He cleared his throat and tried again, "Dad?"

His father lifted his head, startling Jeff with the concern in his expression, the fatigue in his eyes and the heavy lines of disappointment turning down his mouth.

And then it all came back.

"Dad, I…" What could he say? How does one live with oneself after taking another's life? He could still see Carlos's wide-eyed surprise when he'd realized Jeff had come to and made it out of the crate. Carlos had raised his gun. Anger had seized Jeff and this time, he didn't fight it. With tight-fisted determination, he pointed Willa's gun and fired.

Kill or be killed? Had he made the right choice? Or had he succumbed to the anger he'd always kept at bay? Was there even the slightest chance he could have survived? What if he hadn't gone against everything he'd always stood for and taken another man's life? Would he have made it? Did it matter?

He killed a man.

"How are you feeling, son? I'm worried about you," his father asked.

"Did Willa call you?" Willa. He vaguely remembered her standing over him, blood splattered across her shirt. The image wound his insides into a knot. How could she face such ugliness day after day?

"No, Officer Pete O'Donnelly did. He assured me you were fine, but I came immediately. Had to see for myself." Something cracked in his voice.

Jeff looked up in surprise.

"I came real close to losing you tonight. I guess I've been sitting here thinking about the choices you've made—"

"I know it's going to be real hard to live with what I've done—"

"What you've done?" Exasperation shortened his breath, and drew the furrows deeper into his forehead. "You got yourself involved with a woman hip-deep in bad news. You let her drag you into this mess and now you're going to have to find a way to clean it up and extricate yourself."

Jeff choked. Willa wasn't bad news; she was a hero. She fought the good fight day after day and had somehow managed to come out unscathed. But she was right; their worlds were too different. *They* were too different. He didn't know if he would be able to bounce back this time, didn't know if he should.

"You have bloodstains on your soul, son, and

frankly I'm not sure how you're going to live with the choices you've made.'' His father rose.

''I'm sorry, Dad.'' Sickness twisted and turned within him. ''I didn't know what else to do.''

''As any parent, I tried to shelter you from the evil in this world.'' He blew out a deep sigh, the exertion adding yet another line to a face full of creases. ''But try as I might, you kept going back to her like that proverbial moth to the flame and, this time, son, your wings got burned bad.''

That they had, Jeff agreed. Along with his will to fly.

The next morning, Willa stared into her cup of tea, wondering what she should do. For the first time in years she had nothing to focus on. With Jack behind bars and Carlos dead, there were no bad guys in her crosshairs.

Now what?

Now she had to concentrate on building the life she'd put on hold for so long. And she wanted a life. A new life. And finding a new job was the first step she needed to take. She was tired of the dirt and the lies. She wanted to focus on the positive. Maybe then…

''Here, honey. You need to eat something.'' Margo slid a slice of banana bread in front of her.

''Thanks, but you don't need to sit here with me. I'll be fine. Go take care of Ben.''

''Humph.'' She swatted at the air in front of her. ''Ben's got enough people fussing over him. It's you I'm worried about.''

"I'm fine, really," Willa answered automatically. "I'm just contemplating making a few changes in my life." But she knew it would take a lot more than a career change before Jeff would ever want to be with her again. It would take a complete personality transformation.

"Is he worth it?" Margo asked, raising one perfectly sculpted eyebrow.

"That and so much more." Willa sighed.

"Then what are you waiting for? Do you think lightning strikes twice in this life? When you've landed a golden goose you don't just let him leave. Go after him before he lands in some other lucky lady's lap."

Willa blinked. "You think?"

Margo threw the pot holder, hitting Willa square on the head.

"Okay." She laughed, and took a bite of banana bread. Should she go after Jeff? A rush of excitement coursed through her at the thought, but it was a terrified excitement and she wasn't sure she had the courage. She'd made it perfectly clear how she'd felt. He'd rejected her, leaving her alone in the Jeep to go after Tracey—an extremely foolish move, but one that paid off.

"Do I think? Land's end, girl. Do you think Ben and I just fell instantly, madly in love and it was smooth sailing from there?"

Willa smiled. "Yes."

Margo leaned across the table and looked her square in the eye. "Love is hard work, ain't no two ways about it, but it's a labor of love and well worth it.

Now go pretty yourself up and nab that man before he slips away.''

''I don't know...'' Willa stalled. ''I'm sure he never wants to see me again.''

''Willa Barrett, I've never known you to be scared of anything, and here you are too chicken to follow your heart.''

Willa had to grin. ''It's not fair that you know me so well.''

''I also know what's good for you, so get a move on.''

Willa relented, and thirty minutes later pulled into the hospital parking lot not sure what she'd say when she found Jeff. Perhaps she'd just beg for his forgiveness for putting him in such a horrible situation. As a civilian, he never should have been there. She only hoped he'd be willing to give her—to give them—a second chance.

With each footstep down the hall, her strength grew. She was doing the right thing, for her and for Jeff. No matter what it took, she would make him see that. She was practically running by the time she reached his floor. She saw his door open and hoped his father wasn't still there. This was a confession she wanted to make alone.

She loved him, and she wouldn't live without him.

She turned into his room, anticipation swelling in her chest and found his hospital bed empty—the sheets already changed, fresh blankets pulled taut.

''Can I help you?'' A nurse asked, entering the room.

"I'm looking for the patient that was in this room. Jeff MacPhearson?"

"The minister?"

Willa nodded.

"The doctor released him an hour ago."

"Oh," Willa said, disappointment dropping her smile.

"Any idea where he might have gone?"

"Home, I think."

Willa sped toward Pasadena, mulling over in her mind all the things she would say, the words she would use to try to convince him she was wrong. She could fit in his world, and he in hers, because she was ready to face everything he'd been trying to tell her. She was ready to change her life.

Willa pulled into the rectory parking lot and ran through the rose garden toward the offices. She didn't have a clue where Jeff lived, but perhaps she could convince the receptionist in the church's office to help her find him.

"He's not here, ma'am."

Help me out here, Lord. You've brought me this far, don't fail me now. "But couldn't you just give me his address, it's imperative that I speak with him."

"I'll be happy to take down a message." The young girl with an irritatingly bright smile wouldn't budge. Willa wanted to leave a message, but wasn't sure what she would say. "Call me," sounded too pathetic.

Addled by indecision, she left the office feeling more unsure of herself than she had in years. Jeff, where are you? she thought. She wandered for a few minutes and, before long, found herself standing in front of the thick, oak doors of the sanctuary. Jeff's sanctuary.

Tentatively she walked in, her footsteps silently treading a runner covering Spanish red tiles. Row after row of gleaming pews shone golden, blue and red in the stained-glass filtered sunlight.

Willa took a deep breath. It was beautiful, welcoming and peaceful—not at all like she'd expected a church to be. She didn't feel uncomfortable; in fact, quite the opposite. She shook her head. She'd been such a ninny. She would find a way to make it up to Jeff, if only he let her.

She sat in the front row, her gaze resting on the large wooden cross hanging above the altar. She quieted her mind, deeply breathing in the rose-scented air, and letting herself relax in a way she never had before.

Please, Lord, help me find a way to prove to Jeff that I'm worthy of his love. Help Jeff find it in his heart to trust that what we have is real. I won't disappoint him, not ever again. I promise.

Willa smiled as her heart filled with warmth. Suddenly she knew exactly what she had to do.

Willa stood in Pastor Mike's office, hands on hips, frustration rising in her voice. "Mike! I can't wait any longer, not another minute."

He smiled, his eyes crinkling with amusement. "Patience, Willa."

"Patience! It's been two weeks! I ought to be nominated for sainthood, I've been so patient."

''He's having a hard time dealing with everything that happened.''

His gently spoken words stung Willa's guilty conscience. ''All the more reason for you to get his butt, er...rear down here. We can help him so much better than his father can.''

''Oh?'' Mike asked his eyes widening with surprise.

''Come on, his dad's a stuffed shirt, admit it.''

''Are you saying you care for Jeff more than his own father?''

''No, of course not,'' Willa answered quickly, then chewed on her bottom lip. ''Well, perhaps just a tad bit more,'' she answered gesturing with her thumb and forefinger pinched together.

Mike laughed. ''Admit it, you're hooked and going down.''

''Stop it,'' she cried. ''I just want to speak with him and he won't take my calls and he won't return my messages and if I don't see him soon, I'm going to go truly stark-raving mad.''

''All right, all right,'' he surrendered, raising both hands above his head in defeat. ''We can't have that. I'll give him a call and see what I can do.''

Willa beamed with relief and gratitude. ''It's about time, but Mike?''

''Yes?''

''Don't tell him I'm here.''

Mike's bushy eyebrows practically disappeared beneath his thick head of black curls.

''He might not come if you do,'' she responded without taking a second to breathe.

Mike nodded. She took a quick breath of relief and

disappeared before he had time to change his mind. Jeff would come. He wouldn't come for her, but he'd come for Mike. A dull ache squeezed her insides at the thought, but he'd come and she'd have to be happy with that. It would be her chance to prove she was making a different life for herself. One that embraced God's light, and included friends and family. She wanted Jeff to be a part of that life—a big part.

Jeff slowly replaced the receiver in its cradle. Mike had finally called. He'd have to face what he'd been putting off for the last two weeks. He'd have to make a decision.

He'd been living in a state of limbo, trying to come to terms with what he'd done. He'd asked God for guidance and forgiveness, and to help him to choose the right path. But confusion had clouded his vision. That and a lonely ache in his heart that just wouldn't lift.

He went over that night again and again on the drive to Sun Valley as he had so many times in the last two weeks, trying to determine what he could have done differently, what he could have changed.

He realized suppressing his anger over Dawn's death, over the injustice that criminals like Jack Paulson were out there victimizing people every day had been a mistake. Instead of letting it go, he'd been pushing it down, letting it build until finally he exploded. He should have faced it and given his anger to God.

He had to come to terms with his anger, face it,

then let it go before it destroyed his life. What life he had left.

He pulled into the parking lot and killed the ignition. He should have taken his chances with Carlos's bullet. He was dead now anyway. He certainly wasn't fit to be advising and guiding children. The weight of his troubles was too heavy for his shoulders as he walked toward Mike's office. He knew what he must do, knew what he had to do, and he was afraid the sorrow permeating his whole being would be too apparent to his old friend.

"Hello, Mike," Jeff said, forcing a smile on his face as he walked into the cluttered office. "I'm sorry I haven't come sooner. I realize I've left you hanging."

Mike nodded, his steady gaze boring into Jeff's conscience.

He can see right through me.

"I'm sure you've heard the news about what happened a couple weeks ago in the warehouse district," he started.

"Yep, sure did. Real sorry about that. Tough break." Mike drummed his fingers on the desk, refusing to release Jeff from his intense scrutiny.

"Yeah," Jeff agreed. "Doesn't get much tougher. I'm afraid—"

"But you did the right thing, saving that girl and her mom. You're a regular hee-ro." Mike grinned and leaned back in his chair.

Jeff choked on his surprise.

"You're a brave man, Jeff, a man who put himself in jeopardy just to save others. That's the kind of selfless act we need to have more of in this world."

Jeff didn't know what to say. In fact, he was stunned into speechlessness.

Mike rose, came around the desk. "We'd be proud to have you come back home to us. In fact, if you don't mind, we're a bit shorthanded here tonight. We could sure use your help serving dinner to the homeless. Would you mind? I have something urgent I have to attend to."

"No, not at all," Jeff said, still trying to comprehend what had just happened.

Mike patted him on the shoulder. "Good. You remember the way?" he asked and led him toward the door to the fellowship hall.

Jeff nodded and watched Mike disappear down the hallway. Reluctance fell upon him as he grasped the doorknob. He was afraid of the condemnation he'd see in the eyes of the kids; kids he was supposed to set an example for, kids he was supposed to help.

He took a deep breath and pulled open the door.

Willa.

As if an invisible hand gave him a mighty whack, the sight of her standing behind the service counter knocked the air clean out of his chest. His eyes soaked her in as she spooned mashed potatoes onto people's plates. She must have felt him staring, for across the crowded room her gaze fixed on his, knocking a wallop to his already aching heart.

Willa, his mind whispered. Had she always been so beautiful? That stubborn red curl that refused to stay confined slipped out from under a blue scarf and trailed down her cheek. Her lips quivered into a small smile. He tried to walk toward her, but his feet wouldn't move. What was she doing there?

"Come on, Jeff," Jeremy called. "You gonna help?"

Jeff nodded, but was unable to tear his gaze from Willa. He moved into the room, crossing the floor and stepping behind the counter. He'd have no choice but to talk to her. There would be no escaping her this time.

"Hi," she said, smiling at him. A beautiful smile that could melt the polar ice caps and was doing quite a number on his frozen heart. "How have you been?" Her eyes searched his like two high beams, probing.

"Okay, I guess." He heard himself speaking the words, but had no idea where they'd come from.

"I've tried to call," she said.

He could see the hurt and disappointment in her eyes. "I know." He should have taken her calls. He didn't know why he hadn't except that he'd felt so ashamed. And now he felt like a heel.

Gently, she touched his arm. "I—I've left the department."

"What?"

"I want another chance, Jeff. I never should have dragged you into my world. You are too good—"

"You left the department, for me?" Disbelief coursed through him. "You can't do that. I wouldn't want you to. I wouldn't want that responsibility."

"It was the right decision," she said adamantly. Her gaze focused steadily on his, imploring him to understand.

He didn't. How could he? "You loved being a cop."

"No, I didn't. I realize that now. I was never happy, but now I am. I'm doing something good and worthwhile here, something for me. It feels right."

"I'm sorry, I don't understand."

"It's okay. Here—" She handed him the gravy ladle and turned her attention back to the potatoes. She chatted easily with the people she served, even calling them by name.

When had all this happened? How?

Plate after plate, she'd scoop out the potatoes and he'd top them with gravy. More than once, their fingers would touch, their eyes would lock. She'd smile and his heart would ache. Had she really given it all up for him? She shouldn't have. He could never be the man he was before, a man worthy of her.

"I'm sorry." He dropped the ladle and quickly left the room.

Willa's hope plummeted as she watched Jeff hurry from her side. "Jeff wait," she called. She couldn't let him go now; if she did, then she'd lose him forever. She removed her scarf and apron and ran out of the room, but Jeff was nowhere to be seen.

"Jeff," she called. "Jeff!" She ran through the building, the parking lot, the grounds, and finally realized where he'd gone.

Quickly she made her way to the sanctuary, her heart pounding with each step. This was her last chance. *Help me out here, Lord,* she prayed and silently entered the church.

Jeff sat in the front pew, his head bowed in prayer.

She slipped onto the bench beside him, her heart throbbing with his pain, and with her own. She'd done this to him; she'd let this happen. She pulled the whistle out from under her shirt and blew softly. He lifted his head and looked at her, anguish filling his eyes.

"I need you," she whispered.

"I can't. I'm not the man I used to be."

"You can," she countered and pulled him into her arms. For a second, she felt him resist before succumbing and burying his head in her neck. She held him tight, relishing their closeness, his warmth. After a few minutes he straightened and looked her in the eye.

"You don't need me. You're strong and you know exactly what you want and how to get it. You're a wonderful person."

"Not without you, I'm not."

Surprise filled his eyes. "How can you say that?"

"You believed in me when no one else would. You taught me to believe in myself and to trust in God. You saved my life, my heart, my soul."

Her words wound around his heart and squeezed. "I wish I were all that."

"You are."

She sounded so sure, and he wanted to believe so badly.

Her hand rested on his arm. "I know you're having a hard time accepting your role in Carlos's death—"

"I killed him, Willa. You can say it, you should say it."

"All right. It's true. You killed Carlos. And because you killed Carlos, Tracey, Evelyn, Ben and I, we all lived. We all lived because of you and what you did for us. We can never repay you for that, we can only hope you can forgive yourself and accept our love and our gratitude."

Emotion burned inside him. If only he could let it all go and accept her love. He wanted to more than anything. *Because he loved her.* The thought, so unexpected yet so right, spread warmth and hope surging through him.

She touched his cheek, her warm fingertips lingering. "You once told me that I was God's gift to Tracey. But it was you, Jeff. God's gift to all of us was you."

He wrapped his arms around her, pulling her close. Her heartfelt words healed him like balm on an open wound.

"I love you," he whispered.

"I love you, more," she answered and tears filled her eyes, spilling over and running down her cheeks. He kissed away her tears, moving gently over her eyes, her cheeks, to rest on her lips. Warmth surged through him at her softness. She clung to him, each grasping onto the strength and the healing power of their kiss.

He knew she was the one he'd been waiting for, the answer to his prayers, the woman who would make him whole and make his life complete. With her, he would be able to face his anger and learn how to forgive himself.

Thank you, Lord, for helping me find my path, and for putting me on a collision course with a disaster in spandex named Willa—my life, my everything.

Epilogue

"Do you think he'll come?" Willa asked. "I did my best to win him over. To explain how much we mean to each other, to describe our work here at Sun Valley."

Margo's smile was sympathetic. "He'll come around in time."

"I'm afraid Jeff will be heartbroken if his father isn't here to share this day with us."

"Jeff wouldn't want his problem with his father to put a damper on your wedding. Now come on, time's a wasting."

Willa smiled and fussed with her veil in the mirror, scowling at a stray curl that refused to stay pinned up.

"There," Margo said, finishing with a final tug and pat. "You look beautiful."

"Thank you," Willa murmured softly, though she found herself distracted.

"Don't worry. Everything will be perfect, with or without Jeff's father."

"I hope so." Willa sighed and once again looked at herself in the full-length mirror. She was really doing it. She was getting married and not to just anyone, but to the man of her dreams. She smiled, and resisted the urge to pinch herself.

A knock sounded at the door before it opened a crack. "Is it safe to come in?" Ben asked.

"Absolutely," Margo said with a wide smile.

He opened the door, then froze as he took in Willa's reflection in the mirror. "Whooeee, look at you."

"Can you believe it?" she asked, beaming. "I'm not sure I do."

"I always knew you had it in you." He held out his arm. "Are you ready?"

"I think so. Has Jeff's dad arrived yet?"

He looked grim and shook his head. "Sorry, sweetheart."

She sighed. What would it take? What would she have to do to bring Jeff and his father back together again? Life was hard enough not having a father, but to have a dad alive and well, but choosing to stay out of your life had to be more painful than she could even imagine. She looked at the man who'd tried so hard to be a father to her, to make up for what had happened to her dad. "Ben?"

"Yeah?"

There was so much love in his eyes when he looked at her. How could she have been so blind all these years? She drew her upper lip into her mouth, trying to ebb the flow of tears rushing into her eyes. "Thank you, so much," she said through a throat constricted with emotion.

Concern flooded his face. ''Whatever for?''

''For being here. For being my dad.''

''Honey, I love you. I always have. Walking you down the aisle is the best gift anyone has ever given me.''

Her futile effort to keep her emotions in check failed and tears spilled over onto her cheeks. ''Not just now, always. You've always been there for me.''

''I always will.''

She hugged him, squeezing him tight, then let loose a shaky laugh. ''Now you've done it, you've gone and made me cry and spoil my makeup.''

''You look even more beautiful without makeup,'' he said on a shaky voice and pulled out a handkerchief.

''You mean with it smudged down my cheeks?''

''Here,'' Margo said, and took the handkerchief. Quickly and expertly, she fixed Willa's face.

''Now you'd better fix your own,'' Willa said and started to laugh at the twin lines of mascara running down Margo's cheeks.

Margo smiled and hugged her. ''We are so proud of you. I don't think we'll ever be more, not even when you give us a grandchild.''

Willa raised her eyebrows in surprise, then contemplated the idea. ''Okay,'' she said slowly. ''But how about if I get used to the idea of being Mrs. Jeff MacPhearson for a while first?''

''You got it, kiddo,'' Ben said with a wink, then led her into the church.

Willa barely heard the music as she walked down the aisle, her arm clutched in Ben's. Everyone was standing to greet her, smiles lining their faces. She saw Pete and Johnny, and several officers from the department. It warmed her heart to see them there, wishing her the best.

Jeff stood at the front of the aisle, watching her come toward him, light shining in his eyes. The smile on his face was all the encouragement she needed to take this bold new step into a new world, into his world. Tears once again sprang into her eyes, wetting her lashes. *Thank you, Lord.*

The sun moved from behind a dark cloud, letting a ray of light shine through the stained glass and into her path. She walked into the bright colors, knowing she was leaving the darkness behind her. Surrounded by friends and family and the light of God's love, she'd never been happier or more fulfilled.

She took Jeff's outstretched hand, squeezed it and brought it to her cheek as they stepped up to the altar.

Dear Reader,

I hope you enjoy Jeff and Willa's journey into the dark shadows of today's society. Our Lord never promised us life's path would lead us through a rose garden. But He did promise when the path got too difficult to bear, He would be there to help us cope, to help us find our way. "Trust in the Lord with all your heart and lean not on your own understanding; in all your ways acknowledge him, and he will make your paths straight." (*Proverbs* 3:5-6).

Jeff and Willa will need a little *Luck and a Prayer* to help them through their journey. They will also need to put their faith and trust in the Lord. "Don't be afraid; just believe...." (Luke 8:50). Accept His hand and take a walk with Jeff and Willa through the Sequoia National Forest, where anything can and does happen in "God's Country."

Cynthia Cooke

HEARTWARMING INSPIRATIONAL ROMANCE
Love Inspired
A BABY FOR DRY CREEK
JANET TRONSTAD